THE CITY OF THE SUN

Borgo Press Books by BRIAN STABLEFORD

THE CITY OF THE SUN

DAEDALUS MISSION, BOOK FOUR

BRIAN STABLEFORD

THE BORGO PRESS

MMXII

THE CITY OF THE SUN

FIRST BORGO PRESS EDITION

Published by Wildside Press LLC

www.wildsidebooks.com

THE CITY OF THE SUN

CONTENTS

CHAPTER ONE

Nathan was drumming his fingers on the tabletop, just to keep himself active. He was irritating the rest of us, but if he'd stopped someone else would have started. It was one of those times when a state of mild irritation is preferable to deadly silence. I had a sheaf of papers in front of me, and was pretending to study them earnestly, but I wasn't fooling anyone. At least I was putting up a better show than Linda Beck, who was staring studiously at a purely hypothetical object somewhere above Conrad's head. Conrad had his eyes half-closed, in a fashion that suggested both tiredness and diffidence.

Mariel, meanwhile, was watching us all, absorbing our anxiety, our impatience and the tautness of our thoughts, but without relieving us of any of the burden. For once, her talent didn't give her any meaningful advantage. We could all read one another's minds, and know what was going on therein. We were, for once, in harmony.

Karen appeared in the doorway.

"We're over dayside again," she said. "The IR scan picked up nothing significant on the nightside. Just a few hot rocks."

"How low are we?" asked Nathan.

"Low enough and still decaying," she replied. "Anything where more than a hundred people might live ought to show up on the photoscan this time around. We can't take in the whole surface but we'll loop all the northern temperate sites that are daylit on this sweep. We did all the southern ones last loop, and if there'd been anything there we'd have spotted it. If they've built anything at all we'll find it now."

She disappeared back into the bowels of the ship. Nathan's fingers, which had paused while she spoke, resumed tapping.

"You could cross them," I suggested. "It might not help but it wouldn't make so much noise." As a conversation-opening gambit it left a lot to be desired.

He stopped drumming. His face didn't change expression and he didn't answer.

Deadly silence.

I was tempted to start my own fingers dancing, but felt that it might be undiplomatic.

Nobody said *"What if...?"*

This was the fourth time around, and we hadn't yet found a colony that was extinct. But Kilner, who'd taken the *Daedalus* out on her first tour, had. Conrad had been with him. We all knew what if...and the prospect gave us cramps in our stomachs. No reply to our signal. No hotspots on the nightside. If nothing turned up dayside...then the colony was dead. Our mission would change. We wouldn't be ratcatchers any longer. We'd be ambulance-chasers. Picking up the pieces, trying to gain something meaningful. from an analysis of what went wrong. It wasn't a job that anyone could look forward to.

If....

We'd have to land at site prime and start searching. We'd search for a year if need be. If they'd missed the site by a long way, we'd find nothing. They could have come down in the tropics or in the ice fields...somewhere that simply didn't leave them a chance of survival. Unless the scan picked up wreckage, we'd never know. If they were nearer site prime—practically anywhere in the temperate zones—then we'd pick up *something.* We'd be able to spot changes in the vegetation left by any kind of human interference.

Even a crashed ship.

Somewhere inside me a callous voice was adding up the score. *A dead world here is only a second failure,* it was saying.

Along with Dendra. The score's still level. The voice was an idiot. We weren't playing games. And the score would have to be decided on factors a lot more complex than plus or minus. We were dealing with critical thresholds—the most critical one of all being the one that would decide whether the UN thought the gamble of re-mounting the colonization program worthwhile. Within the little voice was another little voice which said: *It'd be best to find nothing at all. If the ships never got here it was their fault. A mechanical failure. Not an argument against the program. The next best thing to a successful colony is nothing at all.*

That second voice wasn't such an idiot. But it was a thorough-going bastard. I didn't want to listen to it.

Karen's voice came over the intercom. "They're going through the computer now. There's a microfilm reel recording automatically. If the computer spots anything we can look at it right away. If it doesn't—well, we can check by eye, just in case."

Just in case. I let the words echo in my mind.

"Six minutes to site prime," said Karen. "Forty minutes before we're back into the black."

"Forty minutes," murmured Nathan.

It sounded a long time. It *was* a long time. But we were low, now, and moving slowly enough for the heatshield to cope. Once we were back into the shadow we'd have a long wait *knowing* that nothing would show up on the IR. Then another long pass over daylight, taking in the southern sites. No more chances after that.

I looked hard at Conrad. Underneath his mask there was genuine fatigue—the fatigue of long and constant strain. He was getting old...but he was aging faster than he had any right to. The strain was taxing him. Our job wasn't the kind of thing that you get used to. It starts again every year. A different world, a new situation, a new set of problems. The *modus operandi* might be the same, and a lot of the drudge work was as mechanical as digging holes in the road—biochemical analysis, nucleic acid synthesis, operon modification...miracles all, but routine miracles, with all the fast work done by computer and only the slow, slow thinking left to human minds. But still, after all that, every job was different. Every world had something unique, something different to throw at us. And no world went out of its way to make it easy for us to cope. It was never easy.

Conrad saw me watching him. He raised a hand slightly in acknowledgment. I looked away.

The minutes dragged. Time in slow motion. The moving finger writes, and having writ...slows down. Pauses. Moves on... but slowly, painfully.

Karen's voice, distorted by a slight buzz on the intercom, said: "We have a hold. The computer's holding. I'm snatching the reel to isolate the frame. I'll get it on the screen in half a minute."

Nathan's fingers beat a brief, exultant tattoo. *One, two, three, four, five...once I caught a world alive.*

I had to swing in my chair to fix my eyes on the screen. Nathan leaned forward, and I could feel his breath on my neck.

The photograph came up.

"Left of center," said Karen.

There was a thin ribbon of grey. A peculiar broken effect that meant hills to the top right and bottom left. Patches of white along a seacoast—white sand and chalk cliffs—which took a bite out of the lower right corner of the frame. A river estuary curved in to the center of the field, and just left of center began a contoured polygon of cultivated land. Not a vast acreage, but quite clear.

And in the center of the polygon was a tiny circle.

"Blow-up coming," said Karen.

The picture clicked, and the central area expanded. There was considerable loss of definition—the land around the circle became blurred—but the circle itself remained quite clear, and showed up as a series of circles, each within the other. Concentric circles, like an archery target. I tried to count them, but only the outer three or four were clear. The inner ones were blurred, and the picture was complicated by the fact that there were patches of white in between the circles, irregularly distributed. There were more than five rings, but less than ten.

Like a cross-section through a branch, I thought. *Growth rings. A city with growth rings.*

"A circular city," said Nathan, softly. "Like the City of the Sun."

"What?" asked Linda.

"One of the classical Utopias," contributed Conrad.

"A city with seven concentric walls," said Nathan. "An impregnable city, with all the knowledge of the world inscribed on its walls. Perfect knowledge and total commitment. Seventeenth century, I think. Written by Tommaso Campanella while imprisoned by the Spanish Inquisition."

"Are there seven?" asked Linda, with what seemed to be unwarranted pedantry.

"It makes a sort of sense," said Nathan, ignoring the mundane question. "After all, they came here in search of Utopia. They came determined to build one. Why shouldn't they adopt the physical plan of one of the classics? A gesture, I suppose. They can't, of course, have adopted the social system...somewhat out of date, I feel."

Karen appeared again in the doorway to take a look at the blow-up. Her question, too, was definitely down-to-earth.

"Alive or dead?" she said.

"Alive," said Nathan, a little more positive than he had any right to be. "That city wasn't built in a day. The colony's only been here a hundred years, and that looks like a hundred years' worth of work to me."

"What's its diameter?" I asked.

Karen stepped over to the image on the screen and measured the circle against her thumbnail. Then she paused for rapid calculation.

"Eight miles," she said. "Give or take a couple, allowing for the blur. Couldn't get a better image, you see—too much water vapor in the low atmosphere. If the cloud cover was much worse we'd have had to rely on indirect information only the computer could handle. You're lucky to get this."

"Thanks," said Nathan, dryly. "I'm sure we all appreciate your technical expertise."

"I'm not," she muttered.

"If there *are* seven walls," I said, "there's about half a mile in between them. And they're thick walls, to show up so well under such difficult conditions." I paused to glance at Karen, who merely raised her eyes to the ceiling. "Anyhow," I went on, "it's no metropolis."

"Eight miles across is a pretty healthy size," objected Nathan. "And the walls needn't be solid. You could pack a lot of people into that little area. Without the use of skyscrapers."

The tension had all evaporated now. We were babbling for the sake of it. All the speculation was futile, considering that we'd be landing to make contact before the day was done. We had a place to land, now. We'd found our needle in the haystack. And even if they didn't answer our signal, they were probably alive and well.

There were plenty of tragedies that we might find yet, but the worst one of all was averted, and we all felt good.

One of the old Utopias, I thought. *A gesture.*

I liked that. It was evidence of a certain panache on the part of the colonists. After all, Utopia was what the game was all about. A new life in the stars. A better world, to build up from scratch, avoiding all the mistakes that history had made on Earth.

All the avoidable ones, anyhow.

If there *were* any avoidable ones.

They had named this world Arcadia. They had a little list of nice names for nice worlds, and when the survey teams came back they even had a committee to sit down and choose one that might—just might—be a little more appropriate than the next. It was basically a publicity stratagem. *Emigrate to Arcadia* sounds a hell of a lot better than *Emigrate to Fingleton's World.* Fingleton had been captain of the scout-ship which did the preliminary atmosphere observations. His name was no worse than anyone else's name (well, not much) but it didn't quite have the charm of Arcadia. Anyhow, it seemed that the human race was condemned to spend eternity expanding into a universe full of habitable worlds with stupid, banal names. Unless, of course, some brave soul took it upon himself to change his planet's name to something like Wildeblood.

On reflection, perhaps there was something to be said for Arcadia.

I got up from the table, feeling that I could now relax on my bunk for a while before the landing.

Arcadia and the City of the Sun, I said, silently. *Here we come.*

CHAPTER TWO

We came down on the flat top of a small hill that was crowned by a tangle of pale vegetation. The external cameras showed us nothing but a great carpet of green dappled with yellow flowers. The vegetation looked to the casual glance like a mixture of gorse and bracken, but somehow *softer.* The plant life in this region of Arcadia—and practically all over the temperate zones—was fleshy and rubbery. Little grew here that was coarse or thorned or thistled, and little enough—according to the survey team—that was poisoned or unpalatable. The image propagated by the survey team was of a gentle world. Also a rather boring one, painted in pastel shades.

The planet had moved on about its axis, as planets tend to do, and we came down in darkness, with the greater part of the night ahead of us. By ship's time it was early morning—three or four A.M. and we'd all been up for a long time. We elected to sleep out the darkness and make a start in the local dawn. It might have been pleasant to go out, even in the darkness, to get a breath of the air and see what there was to be seen with the aid of a lantern, but that would have been stupid.

Pete Rolving had to stay on duty anyhow, so he continued to try to contact the city by radio, but if they still had a receiver functioning they were apparently prepared to ignore the signal.

I doubt that anyone slept a great deal—anticipation and sleep don't mix too well. The imagination can always be relied upon to call up ideas by the score, based on the most inadequate evidence, and few of us have the strength of mind required to tell our imaginative faculties to calm down because the reality will make the speculations redundant in a short enough time. All kinds of notions ran through my mind, conjured up by the city with circular walls...encouraged by the darkness and the stillness and the fact that I was in the borderlands of sleep. My memory kept producing reminiscences of Floria and Dendra and Wildeblood, on all of which worlds we'd had a hard time, at least to start with. But Arcadia, surely, was boring enough to be safe. It had just one marked eccentricity in its life-system—the persistence and evolutionary success of colonial pseudo-organisms alongside metazoan organisms. That, I told myself, was hardly significant. But when the conscious mind descends to the brink of sleep the imagination can follow its own leads. *In the sleep of reason, nightmares come....*

And I couldn't avoid a sense of unease that dogged me through the long night.

We rose at dawn, ate quickly, and made ready for the contact. This was Nathan's area and he took charge, but I volunteered to go with him. It seemed safer for just the two of us to emerge initially from the protection of the ship, and so the rest were left behind to wait for our first impressions.

We stepped out of the lock into a cool, damp morning. There was a slight mist but I judged that it would clear quickly. The sun seemed very large and pale as it clung to the eastern horizon.

The city was hidden from our view by a hill of considerable area but no great height. There would be a long walk down into the shallow valley and up a gentle but extensive slope before we got to the crown of the hill and could look out over the valley in which the city and its cultivated land were situated, along with the river.

The vegetation was knee-deep for thirty meters or so around the ship, but then the yellow flowering plants were less densely packed, and we could pick a way around the worst patches. All the stems were damp, but they didn't cling to our legs as we walked through and over them. Our boots crushed the sap from the shoots and leaves, and wherever we trod we left footmarks that would remain conspicuous for some considerable time.

The only trees we could see were small, thin and short in the trunk but with many thin branches whose leaves were not yet fully developed. The season was early spring. Many of the species were still in their growing phase, not yet flowering— the domination over the aspect of the landscape which the pale yellow enjoyed would not last for long.

There seemed to be very few insects about, but this, too, I ascribed to the time of year. We heard no rustling in the clumps of weed that might have betrayed the presence of small mammals, but the suppleness of the stems probably allowed such creatures to move in virtual silence. A few small birds like skylarks fluttered high in the sky above the hills, sounding high-pitched voices every now and again, but we saw none at close range.

There was a slight moist breeze which gave the morning a slightly raw feeling.

"Very pleasant," I commented.

"They all look nice," replied Nathan, with something less than enthusiasm, "but they all seem to have something lurking behind their smiles."

It seemed that he, too, had been slightly troubled by images on the edge of sleep.

"You could say the same about Earth," I pointed out.

"It goes double for Earth," he said. "Or even more so. If these worlds were no better than *Earth*...."

Once the trace of bitterness had escaped, I felt sure that he'd be back to his old smooth self. "They only called it Arcadia because of this region," I mused. "This world has some pretty fierce deserts around the equator, and whole continents of tundra. I wouldn't call it an evolutionary success story, even by Earth's standards. Not exactly half-hearted, but on the other hand, not wholly hearted, either. Only the sea is really rich with life—oceans like Floria's, shallow and full of weed, swarming with fish. Big herbivores, too—mammals gone back to the sea for preference. Estuarine cattle. If I were them, I'd have stayed on land. Some of the nastiest predators are in the sea."

"I don't intend to do much swimming," he assured me.

"Of course," I added, "there are packs of wolves in the hills. Nobody's entitled to a free and easy life, even here."

We toiled up the vast slope of the hill that stood between the ship and the city. It was very shallow, but we'd been on the ship for three weeks this time—quite long enough to have the edge taken off our fitness. You don't put on fat on ship's food, but it's still easy for your muscles to get lazy. I felt the walk, in my legs and in my breathing. So did Nathan. The top of the hill seemed to retire discreetly into the distance as we approached it.

"Where are the famed colonial algae?" asked Nathan, indicating with an airy sweep of his hand that he couldn't see any close by.

"In the sea, mostly," I told him. "The ones that have come out onto the land are far enough away from the more primitive form not to be describable as algae any more. Even the ones in the sea are called algae only because the colonial mode of organization is limited to the algae back on Earth."

The colonial algae, on Earth, are a kind of evolutionary backwater. A dead end. Why have an assortment of independently viable cells living in association with little more than the beginnings of a division of functional labor, when you can have a multi-celled organism in which genuine specialization of function can be achieved? The colonial forms, which had persisted here on Arcadia, retained a considerable degree of versatility—especially important among parasitic forms—but didn't have a lot to recommend them in terms of complexity or efficiency. They were just a freak of nature that natural selection hadn't gotten around to weeding out. It wasn't that Arcadia was a young world, compared to Earth—in fact, it was somewhat older—but as on virtually all the colony worlds, the tempo of evolution had been different because of the absence of significant tides. Really, it's Earth that's the freak, for being part of a binary system.

"Actually," I told Nathan, "we can see a few of the colonial protozoans. They're just not very obvious. There are tufts that look like little pincushions in the grass here and there."

I directed his attention to the growths in question—no bigger than a fingertip, although each one consisted of millions of individuals.

"I see," he said. Without enthusiasm.

"And the things that look like brown spider webs around the flowering heads here?" I said, this time pointing to the nearest clump of the yellow flowers.

"I thought they *were* spider webs," he said, this time looking a little more closely. "And this one has a spider sitting in the corner."

"Ah," I said. "That one is a spider web. But not this one, see? A nice copy, but a different texture and a lighter color. A fly that gets trapped here is eaten by the web, not by the spider."

"How very economical," said Nathan. "I always thought that spiders could be made redundant, if only nature tried a little harder."

With Nathan, that sort of thing passed for a joke.

"If everything on Arcadia vanished except for the colonial protozoans," I pontificated, "you'd still be able to see everything in ghostly outline. On Earth, the same is supposed to be true of the nematode worms, though no one's actually tried the experiment. Here, parasitic protozoans have a much greater role to play, thanks to the advantages of colonialism. Do you think there's a moral there somewhere?"

"Could be," he said. "If we ever have to fight nematode worms for possession of the galaxy."

"The colonial protozoans are very adaptable," I said. "They don't go in for specialization much. They just crash right on and infect practically anything. They don't worry too much about survey reports and international finance and political priorities."

"I believe you," he said.

Meanwhile, we came at last to the top of the hill, and looked out upon the human world of Arcadia.

The fields were laid out neatly, following the contours of

the hillsides. There were few fences but a number of hedge-rows had been left as windbreaks. The greater number of the planted areas were green with new crops that were yet a long way from fruition. On an exposed southern face of one of the hills there was a series of groves of fruit trees. There were very few animals visible—no grazing herds, just the occasional pair of creatures that looked, at a distance, something like a cross between a yak and a reindeer. It would be difficult to label them by kind, but as they were undoubtedly used for both riding and plowing it seemed logical to dub them oxen. They suited that name far better than they suited the name 'horse,' anyhow.

There were people in the fields, too—several areas were still being planted and others were being combed for weeds. The people were all distant, and mostly seemed to be dressed in simple tunics either white or yellow in color.

But my eye took all that in only for a few seconds. I scanned the scene from horizon to horizon, but the search for detail was cursory as my gaze was dragged back to the one impressive sight—the city.

It was built on a single hill, but like the one we had just climbed it was a large, rounded, shallow hill. It was, I think, too round. No natural hill grew with such geometrical preci-sion. They had sculptured the landscape, moved the earth to create symmetry. Pure showmanship. They had obviously taken their flamboyant architectural gesture seriously. The outer wall seemed quite vast, curving away on either side and then back again, to disappear behind the main, upraised bulk of the city. It was white, and the chalky rock seemed to have been scrubbed clean very recently. It was forty feet high, and thick enough to carry a thoroughfare on its rim. We could see pedestrians, and even riders, making their way around the great perimeter.

We could see almost nothing of what went on behind the walls, but we could see each of the circles rising within one another, telescoped together like a set of cork borers.

Automatically, I counted.

There were seven.

The inmost and highest of all the circles may not have been a wall at all, but we could not see even from our position on top of the hill whether it was roofed over or not. It was too tall—we had to look up to it. It must have been the highest point for many miles. Protruding from somewhere within—or perhaps mounted on top of it—was a thin pylon. I assumed that it must be a lightning conductor.

"It's not as big as Karen claimed," commented Nathan.

"True," I agreed. "She always did tend to overestimate the size of her thumbnail."

"Five miles across," he guessed.

"Maybe less by a few meters," I said. "But you could pack a lot of people into it if you had a mind to. It's built with quite a fair elevation."

As I mentioned people I resumed my scan, picking out individuals in the fields. They were too far away for us to know whether they had seen us. Most of them appeared to be getting on with their work without so much as glancing in our direction.

But we had been seen in the city, at least. Through an arched gate facing us came a group of riders mounted on the "oxen" which seemed to serve every working purpose in the colony. They seemed slightly absurd—almost comical—but in all probability they would have found a horse equally strange, let alone a camel. The steeds did, in fact, cover the ground remarkably quickly. They were deer in the legs and shaggy yak mostly around the back. The males had horns that might have been borrowed from goats or sheep—coiled and ridged.

We continued on our way down the hill despite the fact that the welcoming committee was on its way. We reached the edge of the cultivated land and selected a pathway between the fields. By this time the approaching riders were much closer, and we could see them in more detail. What I saw didn't exactly fill me with enthusiasm. The leader was dark-skinned, and wore a tunic that glittered somewhat in the sun—obviously not made from the same kind of material as the tunics worn by the other people in the fields. His companions seemed to me to be naked, though there was a peculiar black-striped effect visible around the upper parts of their bodies which put me in mind of war paint. This association was considerably helped by the fact that they were all—except the leader—carrying bows, with quivers of arrows slung across their backs.

"Looks like the prince and the palace guard," I murmured. I had slowed down while observing this, and Nathan had to glance back to acknowledge it. By unspoken mutual consent we came to a halt, waiting.

The weird steeds continued their approach, and the black pattern that decorated the naked archers began to stand out even more clearly as a curious network, branching profusely from a center that was gathered about the neck and upper torso. Some of the branches extended out along the limbs to the hands and feet. It looked rather as if someone had drawn a map of the arterial circulatory system on the outside of each man's skin. When they were closer still, I realized that the leader was similarly decorated, although the greater part of the decoration was, of course, concealed by his silvery tunic. His skin was very dark, but its apparent blackness was enhanced by the elaboration of the network around his head and over his skull. I realized that all the men were bald, and that the black pate which each of them boasted was in every case the contribution of the dendritic patina.

Briefly, I looked back over the fields, and even at the pedestrians on the city walls. They were too far away to make me certain, but I felt pretty sure that they, too, owed their dark heads to the same cause.

"I don't think that's paint," said Nathan.

I didn't, either.

Something was growing on their skins—something complex and ordered. The patterns were neatly drawn, the lines were precise. When they came even closer I could see the black stuff—where it was thickest—standing out from the skin in shallow ridges.

There were seven riders in all—six archers and the leader. The six reined in about fifty feet away, jostling for position slightly in the narrow lane. There was only room for two abreast, and they didn't spread out to trample the green corn in the fields to either side. The leader came on alone, the whites of his eyes seeming strangely prominent in the black-capped, brown-skinned face. Two branches extended from the skullcap down between his eyes to run from either side of his prominent nose out into the cheeks, where they subdivided into tiny ramified webs. Thicker lines ran along his brow ridges, substituting for eyebrows. He seemed to have no bodily hair at all. When I glanced at the naked archers to seek confirmation of this impression I couldn't see the slightest trace of pubic hair. But the distance was considerable, and I didn't come to any immediate conclusion.

The dark man's stare seemed distinctly hostile. I let my hands move away from my sides, and I held the palms open to emphasize their emptiness. Nathan did the same, rather more obtrusively.

As the dark man reined in his mount, he asked: "Do you understand me?" His English was slightly accented but otherwise quite clear. What surprised me, though, was the note of his voice. It was very high-pitched. I thought for one moment that I had jumped too soon to the conclusion that he was male.

There was nothing positive, now I came to look more closely, to identify either sex.

"I understand you," said Nathan, in reply to his/her question.

"You are from Earth." It was a statement rather than a question.

"Yes, we are," said Nathan, slightly surprised.

"A bright meteor passed across the sky yesterday," stated the high-pitched voice. "Visible even in daylight. It was your starship."

"Yes," said Nathan.

The man/woman kept the conversational initiative with consummate ease—Nathan never got a chance to develop his sophisticated and much-practiced opening patter. "You must not come to the city today," he/she said. "The Self must be made aware of your coming. You must wait. How far away is your ship?"

"A few miles," said Nathan, "but...."

Buts, however, were not to be allowed. The high-pitched voice cut in quickly: "You must return. If you do not, you will be killed."

That seemed to me to be pretty straight talking. There wasn't a lot of room for negotiation in the statement.

"We must tell you why we have come," said Nathan, quickly. He copied the other's mode of speech easily. When in Rome....

It seemed that Arcadians didn't go in a lot for small talk.

"Tell me now," commanded the man/woman on the beast.

"We have come to help you," said Nathan, compressing his message somewhat. "We set out from Earth three years ago to visit a series of colonies, to find out about their problems and their progress. Yours is the fourth we have visited. Our expertise and the resources of our ship are at your disposal, and any assistance we can offer in overcoming any difficulties you have encountered will be willingly given. My name is Nathan Parrick, and this is Alexis Alexander, our chief biologist. He is a specialist in ecological management. Do you understand all this?"

The other leaned forward slightly as his/her mount dropped its cumbersome head. As the mane parted slightly around the creature's neck I saw traces of black beneath the russet fur. Another black web...just like the one that our interrogator wore. If "wore" was the right word.

Nathan's diplomatic routine suddenly struck me as being slightly stupid. A pleasant, polite rigmarole full of happy assurances and formal greetings. The one question he was really burning to ask he put firmly to one side in the name of protocol.

Excuse me, sir or madam, but why have you got that funny black stuff growing all over you?

To which the obvious answer had to be: *Strange you should ask...I'm desperately curious as to why you haven't.*

In the meantime, he or she had signaled his or her perfect

comprehension of what Nathan was saying.

Nathan went on: "We have also come here to study the colony and its way of life. We have a great deal to learn concerning the prospects of colonies on alien worlds. This is information which Earth needs desperately, in order that the risks taken by future colonists may be minimized. We need to know a great deal about the possible pitfalls and dangers...."

The melodious voice cut in again: "That is enough. You will return to your ship now. A Servant will come to you if you are to be allowed to enter the city. If the Ego permits, then you may put your case to him."

With that, the rider jerked the rein and the beast began to turn away.

"Wait!" said Nathan, quickly. He might as well have been King Canute talking to the tide. The man/woman in the silvery tunic rode back to the archers, who parted to let their leader through, and then turned their own mounts. Not one of them glanced back. They were apparently confident of our compliance.

Nathan stared after them for fully half a minute, and then turned to me. "What...?" he began.

Since everyone else was interrupting him, I thought I might as well get in on the act. "I don't know," I said, quickly. "But we'd better do as he says. Quickly. And no one comes out again without protective clothing. We'll suit up in the lock so that we don't risk carrying anything inside. Isolation. I don't want that stuff growing on me, and if I've already picked up a spore of some kind I don't want to infect everyone else aboard the *Daedalus*. This could be serious."

I was moving even as I spoke. I wasn't particularly worried—I'd been infected with parasites of all shapes, sizes and colors in my time. I'd even picked up alien parasites occasionally during the last three years—ectoparasites aren't so fussy about what kind of flesh they chew their way into. Alien worms and fungi itch just the same as our parasitic brethren on Earth. However, there was a certain niggling anxiety in my mind. This was one hell of a parasite, if appearances could be trusted. And it had no real right to be infecting humans so easily and so copiously as this. The survey team hadn't promised a bug-free world—there are *always* a few local pests that are adaptable enough to bother people—but on the other hand, the survey team hadn't dropped the slightest hint about anything like *this*.

Nathan had to walk pretty quickly to catch up with me.

"You think we might have picked it up already?" be said. "From the air?"

"I'd rather not take chances," I told him. "Black isn't my color. But once we've been through decontamination and suited up, we're as safe as we can be. Let's do that first, and then we'll be free to worry about everything else."

I caught his eye as we marched back up the slope, and I could see in his face that he thought—as I did—that there would still be a lot that warranted worrying about.

CHAPTER THREE

Nathan told the rest what had happened. He told it neatly and economically—but there really wasn't all that much to tell. When he asked me if I had anything to add all I could say was: "It wasn't exactly the greatest first contact in history."

"You were in on it," he pointed out. "I didn't notice your telling contribution."

I smiled, sweetly.

"This parasite...," said Conrad.

"Ah," I said, turning to him. "The matter in hand."

It really wasn't an appropriate time for levity, but I felt the need of a little levity to lighten my mood. I hadn't seen much of Arcadia so far, but what little I had seen I hadn't liked.

"It's obviously not debilitating," said Conrad. "The man who spoke to you seemed perfectly fit and healthy."

"Well," I said—and now I abandoned the levity—"if it was a man, I'd have to be cautious about guaranteeing certain aspects of his health. But if it was a woman, she was probably okay. A flat chest doesn't count as a debility."

"You really don't know whether it was a man or a woman?" asked Karen.

I shook my plastic-sheathed head. "I wouldn't even be prepared to make a statement about the archers," I said. "And they were naked. They were too far away, and they were riding some rather hairy beasts bareback."

"Why should they be naked?" Linda wanted to know. "You say that the people in the fields wore clothing."

That particular guess fell into Nathan's field of competence. I let him take it. "At a guess," he said. "The clothing wasn't so much for protection from the elements as a designation of rank. The one who spoke to us had a garment made out of very distinctive cloth. He obviously had some authority."

"But not all that much," I commented. "He had to report back. To the Ego, and to the Self...which may be the same person or organization, or two different ones."

"Curious names," observed Conrad.

"Ominous names," Nathan corrected him.

I knew what he meant. We could have shrugged off "king," or "master" or "parliament" or almost anything else familiar. Even "metaphysicus" wouldn't have bothered us, because we'd looked up *The City of the Sun* and knew that that was what the top man in the romance was called. But "Self" and "Ego" weren't words you'd normally associate with government, and it had seemed to me that the dark man—or woman—had such a precise way of speaking that it wasn't safe to assume that the terms weren't in some way specifically meaningful.

"It might just be a case of Utopian pretentiousness," said Karen. "These people seem to have gone in for pretentiousness, judging by your description of the city."

"This is a weird one," I said, meditatively, inspecting my fingernails beneath the plastic gauntlet. "I think it might be weirder than we yet imagine."

"Suppose they come back and tell us that they've decided to refuse our application," said Linda. "What then?"

"Well," I said. "It'll be nothing new. We don't exactly seem to be welcome wherever we go. The colonies haven't rolled out a single red carpet so far, although they did give us a good dinner on Floria before they started shooting."

"We've got to find out what's happening here," said Nathan. "Whether they appreciate our being here or not."

"That plastic suit won't stop an arrow," I said, flatly.

"Never mind that," said Conrad. "There's no point in wasting time in speculative meandering when there's real work to be done. For one thing, we have to try to identify this parasite. The survey team probably recorded its presence as a parasite of the herbivores, or some other local species. If we must speculate, let's speculate as to why *they* weren't infected."

"They were only here fourteen months," I reminded him. "And not precisely here, either—we're several hundred miles from site prime...over a thousand, I think. There are any number of versatile parasites among the communal protozoa.... This particular one was probably a good deal rarer where the survey team spent the greater part of their time than it is here. But you're right about identifying it.... Linda—can you feed in the data we have and get the computer to check against the classifi-cation tables? Get it to sort out data cards on anything that fits the basic description."

Linda nodded, and went into the lab to start work on the problem. Once we had the cards codifying the survey team's reports on various suspects we'd be able to get a better idea of what we were dealing with.

The computer didn't take long to do the sort, and it finally belched forth four cards printed with abbreviated jargon. Linda tossed them to me, and I skimmed through them rapidly.

"I was afraid of that," I murmured.

"What?" asked Nathan.

"Here we have four parasites which form black dendritic webs on the outer skin of their hosts. But all four hosts are small mammals of no economic importance or ecological interest. Rabbits and field mice, as near as damn it."

"So?"

"They didn't find it in association with the oxen," I said, patiently. "If they had, they'd have taken a lot more interest in it. The oxen are useful, valuable animals. *Their* diseases were a matter of considerable import in assessing the potential of a colony here—their presence provided a possible source of meat, transport *and* farm labor. But who's interested in rabbits and field mice? The survey team did no more than a routine bioscan on this lot, whereas if they'd found it among the oxen—

from which the people here presumably caught it—they'd have looked at it much more closely."

"Didn't they realize it might infect humans?" asked Mariel.

I shook my head as I studied the cards more carefully, one by one. "They noted that the parasite was probably capable of infecting a range of compatible hosts. They didn't realize how wide a range. But even if they had, they might not have considered it important. Most people, remember, don't just sit back and let things grow all over them. They try to do something about it."

That, of course, was one of the most worrying things. If the people of the city were all infected by this thing then they obviously hadn't put up much of a fight. One of the first things the colonists would have done would have been to prepare some biotic defenses against their new environment. Simple medical technology is the first priority of any colony.

The cards told me that the dendrites ramified internally as well as externally, but only to a limited extent. The bulk of the biomass lay on the surface, with only thin threads—chains of potentially independent cells—linking it to the circulatory system and the nervous system of the host. The parasite was careful not to damage its hosts by too much disruption of the tissues. It didn't feed on tissues—just leeched what it required from the bloodstream. A very considerate vampire, if appearances were to be believed. The surveyors reported that infected animals were at least as healthy as uninfected ones.

Then I saw something on one of the cards that made me put the others aside.

"If anyone wants to bet," I said, "I'll lay six to four on *this* one as the culprit."

There were no takers, but they all wanted to know why.

"It's the special one," I told them. "It has a footnote that the survey team didn't think was especially significant. It says here that this particular species goes in for inductive cellular mimicry. Especially with respect to nervous tissue."

"Which means?" Nathan prompted.

"These communal protozoans are versatile," I said. "It's the key to their success. Some protozoan species on Earth are versatile enough to choose whether to be plants or animals—they can grow chloroplasts and dispose of them as circumstances dictate. The whole essence of communal aggregation is that it's the beginnings of division of labor—some cells specialize in reproduction, others in energy fixation, others in defense. It happens in the colonial algae and in the colonial polyps. The point about communal aggregations, though, is that the cells retain their potential independence—*and* their potential choices. Organisms—multicellular organisms, that is—go in for a much more precise kind of specialization. Once a cell grows to its destined function it remains specialized. Once a liver cell, always a liver cell—the versatility of each individual cell is lost at an early stage in the development of an embryo when cells become fixed into their permanent function. This process of specialization is involved with a mechanism called induction, which causes different tissues to develop in the right places within the embryo in response to the stimuli provided by other tissues developing in the immediate environment.

"These parasites, being communal pseudo-organisms, retain essential versatility in each and every cell. Most of the species don't make a lot of use of that versatility—parasitism is a relatively simple way of life, which doesn't demand a great deal of differentiation of functions. But *this* one is a very highly developed parasite...a super-parasite. You can think of the others as plant-like things, sending tap roots down into the flesh of their hosts to soak up moisture and nourishment. It's essentially a crude business, like drilling oil wells. The parasites are fairly discreet—they use thin drills, strands of cells only two or three thick—but what they do is nevertheless a fairly straightforward job of boring and mining.

"The odd man out is cleverer than that. *His* cells make use of their versatility by mimicking the cells of the host. Thus, when he sends a tap root down through skin tissue to the wall of a blood vessel, the strand cells take on many of the characteristics of dermal cells, and the cells which actually do the thieving take on many of the characteristics of blood-vessel-wall cells. This parasite then has a much higher degree of integration with his host. The host no longer recognizes him as an invader, and thus he becomes immune to the body's natural tendency to reject foreign matter. The *extra* functions fulfilled by these cells—the parasite functions—are masked by the apparent conformity of the cells to their immediate tissue environment.

"I can't tell from this report how far the mimicry goes. But if this parasite is *really* clever—and we have grounds to suspect that it is—then the mimic cells might *actually* carry out the functions of the tissues they mimic, so that as well as the tap root cells being indistinguishable from host-tissue cells by the host's bodily defenses, they actually do the job they ought to be doing if they *were* host-tissue cells. That way, this particular parasite could maintain a much more extensive internal network than its relatives. It wouldn't have to limit itself to a few discreet strands of cells—it could ramify much more extensively inside its host. And that would mean that it could support a much greater biomass all told—something like the formations we could see on these people, instead of just a little thing like a spider web on the back of a rabbit.

"Also, of course, this could explain why the colonists might have been unable to muster any kind of medical defense against this parasite. If its internal ramifications can mimic host cells well enough to fool the host body itself, no external antibiotic would get close to it...not without attacking the host tissues too. The external dendrites—the black cells—are probably fairly easy to dispose of...but if the colonists dispose of them they simply grow back from inside. The roots can't be touched by any normal methods.

"In brief, I suspect that this is the most efficient parasite I've ever come across. Maybe it's so efficient that it doesn't deserve to be called a parasite—maybe just a commensal. It really cooperates with the host body, taking the nourishment it needs with the absolute minimum of biotic vandalism. Maybe the only thing we can say against it is that it isn't very pretty. Maybe...I think I'll reserve judgment on that until I get a much closer, much longer look."

There was a respectful pause.

"You may applaud," I told them.

They didn't. Not that it mattered. I hadn't planned an encore.

"If you're right," said Nathan, "then the obvious question is... can we find any way to attack such a parasite?"

"Oh yes," I assured him. "Genetic engineering gives us much more subtle routes of attack than any antibiotic drug. We can actually attack the thing in its genes—the very genes which give it its versatility and its ability to mimic specialized cells. The parasite cells can only mask their real nature...and we have the means to get behind the mask. It probably won't pose much of a problem to us, if only...."

"...if only we can persuade them that it's a problem," Nathan finished for me. I hated him pinching my punch line like that.

I shrugged. "People do get used to things," I said. "They may not see this stuff quite as we see it. They may like black stripes growing all over them."

"Well," said Linda, with commendable pragmatism, "if the parasite really doesn't do them any harm, they can afford to like it, can't they? And we can afford to let them."

"I think," I said, "that I'd like to reserve judgment on that issue too. Until I've had a much longer and much closer look. I've got this strong suspicion, still, that there's a lot more to this than we've so far guessed."

"Isn't there always?" put in Karen.

CHAPTER FOUR

It was a long day inside the ship, waiting for something to happen. My patience wore pretty thin, not helped by the fact that having to wear a protective suit inside precludes just about every chance you might have of being comfortable. I wasn't convinced that the suit was necessary—it seemed to me unlikely that the parasite reproduced via aerial spores, although communal protozoa characteristically reproduce by fragmentation of the community and binary fission of individual cells. However, with something like this I wasn't prepared to take chances. We had to take every possible measure to protect the rest of the crew from even the smallest risk.

We didn't particularly expect a fast decision, but by the time that Pete announced the approach of strangers dusk was falling, and we felt that they'd overdone it somewhat.

I took a quick look at the screen to see what was happening—it was the same dark-skinned man with what looked like the same six archers in attendance. One of the archers was leading two spare mounts. Behind me, I heard Nathan say: "Suit up, Mariel."

"Is that wise?" I asked.

"Mariel's the best way we have of getting a lot of information fast," he said. "I want to get on top of this one quickly—I want to know just what their attitudes are toward us, this parasite, and life in general."

"They've only brought two spare mounts. Maybe they'll hold us to two visitors."

"In that case," he said, "you stay."

Mariel had paused to hear the beginning of the exchange, but now she set off for the lock to get a suit.

"Oh no," I said. "This is my play as much as it is yours. Those parasites are *my* business...and *I* want to get a line on this just as much as you do. I'm coming in with you."

He ducked the issue. "They probably brought two mounts because they're expecting two of us," he said. "You can ride with Mariel...you're the only one of us who's had practice riding all manner of weird creatures. You help her and I'll manage on my own."

He turned away as soon as he finished, not leaving me space to argue. I cursed silently and followed him, thinking: *At least I get to see how you explain why we're now all dressed up in plastic bags.*

But I was wrong. He didn't explain. He just stepped out of the lock and went to meet our silver-clad friend as if nothing could be more natural than wearing a plastic bag. I watched the dark man/woman's eyes narrow slightly in surprise, but he/she made no reference to the matter. Politeness is a wonderful thing.

"You may come to the city," he/she said. "The Ego will interrogate you. Then the Self will decide whether you are to stay."

Then he/she saw Mariel coming out of the lock behind us.

His/her only comment was: "Two of you must ride together."

The archers were waiting with the spare mounts at the same respectful distance they had maintained during our morning meeting. But now we could approach them. I set off with an eager stride, glancing up at the dark man/woman as I passed his/her placid beast. He/she looked back, his/her face quite impassive and his/her body apparently quite relaxed.

Nathan lagged a few paces behind and fell into step with Mariel.

I heard her say: "Nothing...I can't read anything."

"Stay with it," he said. "Relax and take your time."

Their voices sounded a little hoarse filtered through the vocal apparatus of the suits, which made whispering a little difficult.

My attention was fixed ahead, though. As I came closer to the naked archers I took a good long look at the way the parasite extended itself over the body. I also checked what I hadn't been quite sure of earlier in the day—the absence of pubic hair. The hair was missing, of course...but it wasn't all that was missing.

The archers were all of full adult size—five and a half to six feet tall. They had neither beards nor wrinkles, and it wasn't easy to make a guess at their ages, but none of them were children. But the ones I could see, though definitely male, had sexual organs that were either undeveloped or vestigial. In brief, no balls.

I looked back over my shoulder at the man in the silver tunic. Man he was, I decided. The silvery voice which went with the clothes had simply never broken.

It was something I might have anticipated, at least as one of a number of possibilities, but somehow the thought just hadn't crossed my mind. It came as a shock, now.

I arrived at the waiting mounts, and the archer passed the reins to me. I said "thanks" but he didn't seem to be paying any attention. Now I was close, it struck me what a long way it was from the ground to the ridge of the shaggy back. There was no stirrup to help me up. I'd ridden a lot of animals in my time, including some extremely tall camels, but nothing as weird as this creature. And camels will bend down for you if you ask them nicely.

I passed one of the reins to Nathan and stood back, quite happy to let him take first crack at getting aboard. He'd done most things in his long and colorful life—maybe including riding camels—but when you do just about everything you don't get much practice at anything in particular. I was wondering how he'd go about it.

I should have guessed.

"Give me a leg up, will you?" he said.

I sighed, and let him put his knee into the palm of my hand, then boosted him up. I did the same for Mariel. She took a handful of mane and offered her other hand to me. Somehow, with that assistance, I contrived to end up on the beast's back sitting just behind her. We'd never have managed it but for the perfect docility of the mounts themselves.

I watched Mariel part the mane with her gloved fingers to expose the tracing of black lines against the skin. They were very thin lines, with no gathering at any point into a considerable mass. But on the backs of the archers, I saw, from the base of the neck extending like the silhouette of a bird with wings spread wide, was a large expanse of parasite tissue...a kind of shallow hump.

I wondered, briefly, how a medium-sized creature like a man could support so much parasite, when a large creature like an ox could apparently support so little.

The leader walked his mount back to the group, passing between my beast and Nathan's, and then going through the corridor opened up by the attendants. We followed him, the archers being left to bring up the rear.

"There's something very odd about that man," murmured Mariel, her voice blurring slightly because of the suit.

"Apart from his being a eunuch, you mean?"

She turned slightly, glancing over her shoulder at me. She hadn't picked that up.

"He's got a mind like a brick wall," she said. "I can't read him at all."

"He hasn't got what you might call an expressive face," I agreed. "But give it time."

"It's more than that," she insisted. "There are some people it's difficult to read, sure. I have to be able to look at them for a while, or touch them. The talent isn't like tuning in a radio to people's thought waves. I've met blanks before...but this one is a sort of positive blank. No...that's wrong...don't for God's sake start thinking about mind-shields and things like that. It isn't that kind of thing at all.... Most of what I pick up, you see, is peripheral. It's the fringes of what people say—the things they mutter under their breath, the commentary on their own actions, their unvoiced reactions to what they see and hear. But there seems to be nothing of that in his face. As if his mind were....*still*...completely settled...ordered."

"I saw his eyes narrow," I told her. "When he first saw you. Do you think he can sense your talent? Maybe he...."

"I don't know," she said. "I don't think so. I think that it just didn't fit in with his calculations—three people and two mounts. That's what I'm trying to say about him. He *calculates* everything. Every move, every thought. It's precise. No ragged edges for me to pick up on the borders of verbal communication."

"Mechanical," I said.

"If you like."

"Like a robot."

The mount was walking forward with precisely measured strides. I was just holding the rein limply. The beast knew where it was going. It knew what it was doing. It moved like a machine. A robot.

She couldn't see my face, and there were two layers of plastic between us, but she knew me pretty well by now. She didn't need all the frills to use her talent on me.

"Something's frightened you," she said.

"You're dead right," I told her. "I'm half inclined to duck out of this party right now. I've got a *very* nasty feeling."

I was harboring a thought which struck me as being one of the worst I'd ever harbored. I was thinking that if the parasite cells could mimic all kinds of host cells, that probably included brain cells too. And I was just wondering what might be the implications of a parasite that could turn itself into a mimic of a thinking human brain.

I didn't have to explain to Mariel. She was getting it all by mental osmosis.

"Puppets...?" she said. Somehow, despite the suit, she managed to whisper.

"I don't know," I said. "But *if*...."

My fears piled up like pennies. Only minutes before I'd been prepared to discount the possibility that Nathan or I might have contacted a stray parasite cell drifting around on the morning breeze and it wouldn't have worried me much if I'd found out that I had. But I was worrying now.

Darkness was falling, and that certainly didn't help. Fears always seem worse in the dark. There were a good many stars beginning to peep through in the sky, and the afterglow was dying slowly, but I couldn't see the ground that we were traveling over. The oxen plodded on, absolutely sure of themselves.

"Take it easy," I told Mariel. "The time's right for nightmares. All these ideas are just ghosts oozing out of the dark recesses of my imagination."

"I know that," she said.

"So let's stay calm and look at the situation as it is. Let's not let our fears make prior judgments."

I was talking to myself as much as to her, and she knew that. She didn't resent it.

It took as long to descend the hill on which the *Daedalus* stood and to toil up the long slope to the crown of the next hill as it had in the early morning. Personally, I'd sooner have walked on my own feet than ridden the rather repulsive creatures that had been laid on as transport. But in making contacts there has to be a little give and take, and I suffered gladly for the cause.

I studied the patterns that the stars made in the sky, looking for the brighter lights that were Arcadia's neighbor planets. She had no moons but this solar system was fairly crowded as solar systems go. There was one beautiful evening star, and I picked out one other close by in the curve of the ecliptic across the night sky, but that was all.

When we came to the crest of the hill, however, there was something else to look at. Even in darkness, the City of the Sun commanded attention, shining with a vast array of tiny lights that stretched across its great staggered disk to vanish in the distance.

There were lights on the rims of the walls and lights in the streets, as well as lamps lighting thousands of windows. Most of the lamps were oil-fired, but the lights on the walls were gaslights, burning whiter and brighter. They showed up the white of the walls and made the whole city seem aglow.

"Impressive, isn't it?" I said to Mariel.

"It's so *big*," she murmured. "Did a few thousand people really manage to build that in a few decades? Without heavy machinery...without even any source of power except their muscles and the oxen, and whatever they could improvise."

"You can do a lot in a hundred years," I said. "If you set your mind to it. They had all the resources Earth could give them. No bulldozers, but a lot of suggestions as to how to make do without."

Even so, she was right. It was quite something for a few thousand people to knock together in a few decades, starting from scratch. It must have taken a great many people a great deal of their lives. And all of their dedication and commitment. The colony had certainly gone single-mindedly about realizing its Utopian fantasies. And with the parasites bleeding off all the spare energy the while....

It might not be too good to be true, I thought, but it's surely too good to have been that simple.

There were a few lantern lights bobbing in the fields like will-o'-the-wisps, but it was too dark to see what the people who carried them might be doing. The great majority had finished for the day and gone home. To what? Rest and play.... Or more work?

"I think they're still building it," I said. "I think they'll be building it for a long time to come. The gross work is finished, but *inside*...there must be a long way to go...so much still to be done."

"Especially," she said, "if they *are* writing all the wisdom of the ages on the seven great walls."

"They may be copying the City of the Sun," I said, "but I can't see them taking their model quite *that* seriously."

But as it turned out, I was wrong.

CHAPTER FIVE

The walls seemed to flow and ripple in the unsteady light of the gas lamps and the yellow glow of the multitude of oil-fired lanterns. The outer face of the outermost wall had been smooth, but the outer surface of the second wall was not. As we entered the city through a great gate which opened to admit us and then closed behind us we could look ahead along a wide thoroughfare which led uphill to the second wall and another gate. Around the gate and extending away on either side until buildings blocked our view the wall was decorated with sculpted tiles. Their color was pure white, and from the top of the distant hill, by the diffuse light of the morning sun, they had been quite invisible. But now their lines were etched in shadow, and the wall was completely covered by their "writing."

At first, I thought that they might be abstract decorations, simply for adornment, but as we climbed the hill on our plodding mounts it became abundantly clear that this judgment was ill-made. Each tile was perhaps two feet in diameter—they were stacked twenty deep, and a rough calculation suggested to me that each row probably contained twenty thousand tiles, assuming that they extended all the way around the wall. That made four hundred thousand tiles on this wall alone. There were still five more—albeit getting smaller and smaller in circumference as we neared the center. That added up to a lot of tiles. If there were a thousand stonemasons each carving one a day....

My mind gave up the calculation in favor of boggling. But I knew that no one mounts several million tiles on the walls of his city just so that they're not so boring to look at. If this was art for art's sake these people went in for aesthetics in a very serious way.

At close range, I saw that they were pictographs...highly stylized images. At first it struck me as silly, but then I wasn't so sure. If I were charged with the task of writing all the wisdom of the world on a wall how would I start? Not by starting in the top left-hand corner and copying out the Encyclopedia International from the famous German river *Aa* all the way through to the infamous *zymotic* diseases. In all likelihood, I'd put aside cultural chauvinism and forget phonetic writing altogether. I might use something more like the old Chinese system. After all, they weren't just expert pictographers...they also went in for the building of big walls.

The pictographs weren't the wisdom of the ages, I decided... but they had to be there to *symbolize* the wisdom of the ages. Every picture an idea...and all the ideas that they thought important assembled together, classified and ordered. Not just for decoration, then. A higher aim, of sorts. It sure looked more impressive than a data bank of microfilms and fiches. A work of art indeed.

But why? I wondered.

I couldn't read the pictographs. That was something that would have to be learned—maybe by every child born in the city...if it were humanly possible for a child to learn the secrets of several million pictographs in a few short years. Or even in a lifetime.

Nobody could, I murmured, under my breath.

"Nobody could what?" asked Mariel.

"Learn the meaning of all those pictographs," I said. "It's impossible. What's the use of having all the wisdom in the world written out in the open in letters two-feet high if no single person could ever learn enough to make sense of it all?"

"Perhaps they're not meant to learn it all," she said. "Perhaps it's up there in letters two-feet high to remind them that no one person *could* learn it all—to remind them all how dependent they are on others."

"Why didn't I think of that?" I said, without sarcasm.

"You think it's true?" she asked.

"I don't know whether it's true," I told her, "but it's a neat theory."

We passed beneath the second gate, and entered the second circle. Ahead loomed the third wall, and it came as no surprise to see it tiled in similar fashion to the second. I looked back to see if the inner face of the wall were similarly adorned, but there was no inner face—the buildings of the city grew out of the inner wall, square blocks stacked atop one another in calculated asymmetry, three or four stories high with catwalks connecting the sections of the uppermost level and ladders between levels. It was impossible to say where one building "ended" and another "began"—there were just units in wayward piles. It reminded me strongly of a hollow "artificial mountain" that I'd once seen in a zoo, made for monkeys to live in.

"Think of the time and effort involved in building and decorating those walls," said Mariel. "It wouldn't be a matter of man-hours...whole man-lives. People whose contribution to the colony consisted solely of a few thousand tiles hacked out of soft white stone."

"Not necessarily," I told her. "This may be one of those Marxist Utopias where no one is a sculptor but everyone sculpts. Maybe everyone in the colony has contributed his tile, or his group of tiles. Perhaps they're monuments as well as ideas. A substitute for gravestones. Maybe they are gravestones, and everyone who ever lived in the city is entombed in its walls. We'll find out, in time."

There is a well-known illusion which seems to make the edges of long straight roads converge as you look along them. The main highway of the City of the Sun, however, really *did* get narrower as we went along it. Its pavements really did aim to meet, and not at an imaginary, infinitely distant point but at a point which was geometrically defined with absolute precision—the dead center of the city. As we toiled up the hill, therefore, the buildings drew closer on either side. Through the unglazed windows of the upper stories we could see lamplight reflected from ceilings, but that, alas, was just about all we *could* see of the home life of the citizens. The ground floor units had fewer windows, and these tended to be either dark or curtained. There were no open doors. No one came to the windows to look at the peculiar visitors dressed in plastic bags. Even the people we passed on the road gave us no more than cursory and quite incurious glances. It wasn't that we were being deliberately ignored—just that no one seemed to have any particular interest in us.

"Can you read them?" I asked Mariel.

"I get something," she said, "but it's so vague, so strange. I get the feeling that they all know about us, that we're familiar. I know that gossip spreads fast and the news that we've landed is probably all over the city...but none of them seem to want to know more. They see us, they recognize us, that's it. They seem hardly reactive—not simply to us, but even to the things in their own environment. Look at the way they move, and the way they hardly seem to interact with one another. If they were like zombies that would be more understandable, but I don't think they *are* zombies. They're conscious and aware, I'm sure of it, but their consciousness is so settled, so certain.... Do you see what I'm getting at?"

"If they really *were* robots," I said, "then they *couldn't* think for themselves. They'd be automata. But this automatism is facultative. They could think and react if they wanted to, but they don't. They have no curiosity."

"That's it," she confirmed. "That's what I mean. That's what I get from watching them and trying to read them."

Perfectly ordered minds, I thought. Total confidence in both self and environment. As if....

As if they really *did* know everything.

Not just all the wisdom known to man, but all the wisdom possible. Such total security could only be an illusion. Couldn't it?

"Whatever the parasite is doing," I said to Mariel, "it isn't just sitting on their backs keeping them company. If it *hasn't* taken them over completely—and there's too much here that's human for me to believe that—then it's certainly given them a lot more control over their own minds than we have."

One thing that struck me particularly was the *cleanness* of the road along which our beasts of burden trudged. There were drains set in the angle of the pavement and the road surface itself, protected by stone grilles. The holes were quite small, but they seemed to have collected virtually no detritus. They didn't smell of anything particularly noxious. We were at the end of a working day, on what was presumably the busiest street in the city, used by people, oxen, carts and carriages, but there was no mess.

Orderly minds, I thought, *orderly bodies, orderly habits. Even the yaks are toilet trained.*

I thought of the title of a paper: "Solutions to the Sewage Problem in Classical Utopian States." Knowing the UN, though, they'd never let me publish. They'd classify it secret.

We passed into the fifth circle, and saw that the penultimate wall was as fully developed as all the rest.

"It's not so hot, now I come to think about it," I said. "Every wall in New York has a covering of graffiti six layers thick. And New York is *much* bigger than this place."

"In New York," observed Mariel, "they use spray cans, not chisels."

"Maybe we'd better not talk about this back home, then," I said. "We might give them ideas."

There was hardly any traffic on the road. We passed a couple of ox-drawn covered carts on their way down the hill, but we saw no one else riding, and no carriages. Everyone who was going anywhere was going on foot, and even the pavements were not thronging with people by any means. The incurious pedestrians were all capped in black, and they all seemed to be slimly built. Their heights were various but none was very tall. The great majority of the tunics were white, but I saw a few of the yellow tunics which had seemed most common in the fields. Some wore pale blue, some pale brown in various shades. There was no difference in dress which would have allowed me to differentiate between the sexes...in fact there seemed to be almost no way to differentiate. The tunics were gathered in at neck and waist, but tended to stand out from the body in stiffish folds in between. It wasn't easy to pick out the line of a breast. It should have been a great deal easier to pick out the line of a pregnancy, but I saw none. Of course, it was dark, and the street lighting wasn't particularly efficient. The worst of it was that the crowds were silent. There were no conversations. Like commuters in any city in America or China or Africa or Australia they all passed by without the merest hint of greeting or caring. There was no way for me to measure what proportion of the total population had silvery voices.

It wasn't easy to draw inferences from what we saw.

Eventually, we reached the final circle—the arena within the final wall. Here the gate was closed, and two men dressed in pale green had to emerge from small doors within to haul back the two wooden battens. I half expected to find this innermost circle to be a glorified football stadium with gigantic banks of seating and a small central area where visitors occasionally got fed to the lions. Instead, there were gardens, planted with trees and exotic plants, laid out with a careful and artistic lack of symmetry.

There was a square apron of pavement, where we all dismounted. From the inner face of the last wall grew the same higgledy-piggledy mass of square cells with ladders and balconies and catwalks, but instead of stretching out toward the center it formed only an inner ring—a kind of encrustation on the great white expanse. A few of the people I could see moving on the catwalks were dressed in green—the others were archers.

The mounts were led away to what was presumably a stable—a long, tall rectangular building distinctly different from the human habitations. The man in the silvery tunic led us into the gardens along a path inlaid with mosaic tiles. The archers didn't follow.

There were birds fluttering about in the trees, but they didn't call out. There was no wind to rustle the branches and so the slight, scratchy sound of the moving birds was all that held back the silence. But now the clip-clop of the ox's feet was no longer beneath and around me I could hear faint sounds emanating from distant parts of the city—or perhaps from chambers underneath it. Faint, anonymous, arrhythmic sounds.

In the middle of the gardens—presumably at the geometric center of everything—there was a stone building, shaped like a tetrahedral pyramid but stepped with balconies and gabled windows.

Our guide opened the main door and motioned us inside, then followed us. The ground floor extended the whole way across the building, with no internal walls, though there were three rows of thick stone pillars supporting the rest of the building and two wide spiral staircases. There was no carpet and no chairs, but at the farther end of the huge chamber there were what looked like a series of parallel curved rows of cushions. We didn't get a chance to have a closer look because we were taken to one of the staircases. Still without opening his mouth, the dark man indicated that we should go up.

The first floor had corridors and ordinary rooms. We went up to the second, which was considerably smaller in extent owing to the slope of the pyramid's sides. Here there seemed to be one corridor leading away in two directions, with a set of rooms on its outer side but only one within the inner wall. We were shown into the odd one, and here our guide finally abandoned us, closing the door quietly behind us.

The room wasn't large. It was triangular, with a low ceiling. The three angles of the triangle were curtained off. In the center of the floor was a set of six cushions, arranged to approximate a circle. There was no other furniture save for a low table, on which stood an assortment of crockery. There were four cups— or possibly soup bowls—with handles like pans. There was also a teapot, and a bowl containing some kind of dried fruit. No milk jug, no sugar bowl. A thin wisp of steam was rising from the spout of the teapot.

A man stepped out of the curtains protecting the farthest angle of the room. They rippled together behind him. He looked to be old but well-preserved. He was tall and thin. He had a long neck and a deep jaw, which gave the impression that the top part of his body was elongated unnaturally. The black parasite grew over his skull almost to the brow ridges, and gathered on either side of his neck almost to meet at the Adam's apple. His tunic was black, too, and in the dim light—the room was lit by three oil lamps set in alcoves in each of the three walls—it was difficult to be sure where the garment ended and the growth began. His forearms were bare, and the network of black line seemed to enclose them like extensions of his sleeves. Only his sandals, which were brown, contrasted with the extensions of the parasites. He was brown-skinned, but his eyes had a hint of oriental canthus. His eyes were beady and black.

He moved forward fluidly, seeming perfectly relaxed. There was the ghost of a welcoming smile about his lips.

"Please sit down," he said. He gestured with his hand, not offering to shake Nathan's. Nathan had stepped forward, but quickly altered his movement and sank down rather awkwardly on one of the cushions. I sat on his left, Mariel on his right. Our host took up the position which left a spare cushion to either side of him. I suspected that six cushions had been set out for exactly that reason. I had already noticed that there were four cups instead of three. News had preceded our actual arrival.

"You are the first visitors from elsewhere that our city has ever entertained," said the man in black, as he picked up the teapot and leaned across the table to begin pouring. "We have no customs prepared for such occasions. I am improvising, and I hope not to offend you."

His voice was thin and reedy. I couldn't immediately hazard a guess as to whether he was as underdeveloped as the archers or not.

Nathan reassured him that we were quite unoffended, and introduced himself, then Mariel, and finally me.

"I am called the Ego," said the other. "I have no personal name—I gave that up in taking my place. It has been decided that I should question you. It is necessary that we should know the purpose of your visit."

"May we question you in return?" asked Nathan.

"You may," said the Ego, cordially, "but there are certain answers which I am bound to withhold at this time. I hope that this will not cause offense."

Nathan diplomatically assured him that this was his city, and that we would abide by his decisions.

I tasted my tea. It didn't taste much like any tea I'd ever tasted before. But then, I was taking it in through a multileaf filter and sterilizer. I looked up again to see the Ego watching me. Maybe he'd expected me to take the suit off. Maybe that had been the real purpose of offering us the drink.

Nathan and Mariel were also sipping. Small droplets of the liquid began to dribble down the outer surface of their suits beneath the intake. Drinking through a filter is a difficult art to master—it's easier if you can use specially prepared tubes that squeeze fluid through without wastage.

We ignored the dried fruit, not being able to take solids. The man in black, presumably out of politeness, also left them alone.

While we sipped our clumsy way through a few milliliters of the strange brew, we all looked closely at our host. He looked back, very closely. There was no sign here of the diffidence of the people in the street. I was never so fully conscious of being studied and *measured*. It was as if he were doing all the staring that his people had failed to do—doing it for them. And yet...it wasn't really *curiosity*. There was no wonderment, no eagerness in his gaze. His attitude was purely *analytical*.

"What is your purpose in coming here?" he asked, when the pause had dragged on a little too long for my liking.

"We are visiting the colonies sent out from Earth more than a hundred years ago," said Nathan. "Our task is to find out how they have fared. We also offer certain kinds of help to those colonies which need it. We have a genetic engineering laboratory aboard the *Daedalus*—it can help in adapting crops which have not been successful, in combating pests, in controlling any health difficulties which have arisen. When humans move into an alien environment there are always problems of some kind— usually minor ones. Sometimes the colonists do not realize that the problems exist, or that they can be solved. Thus, we offer help, in return for learning about the ways that you have helped yourselves. Other colonies may soon be sent out, and there is a good deal that you could teach us that may be valuable to them."

It was a pretty enough speech, with some delicate hedging in it. The Ego soaked it all up without changing expression.

"Which nation sent your ship?" he asked.

"The United Nations," said Nathan. "Things haven't changed a great deal since you left Earth—since your ancestors left, that is. No one nation has a space program. The UN combines the funds and efforts contributed by all the nations."

"There is only one Nation here," said the Ego. I could tell by the way he pronounced the crucial word that it had a capital letter—and presumably a capital significance.

"That is as it should be," said Nathan, smoothly. "A colony must remain united if it is to flourish."

The Ego ignored that. I would have ignored it too. A philosophical advertising jingle...a cheap platitude.

"Genetic engineering involves interference with natural processes, does it not?" said the man in black, after another sip from his teacup. I'd abandoned mine, feeling that I'd made the gesture. I didn't like the stuff well enough to drink it for its own sake.

"Genetic engineering can improve crops and destroy pests," I said. "It *is* interference, of course. But agricultural development is itself interference. All the crops your fathers brought from Earth were the products of genetic engineering—manipulated for hardiness and high yield."

"We have a new way of living now," he said, unperturbed.

I wanted to point out that they still had agriculture, but Nathan nudged me to be silent.

"We would like to study your way of living," he said.

"Why do you wear these curious clothes?" asked the Ego, bluntly.

The odd thing was that his voice was perfectly even and unaggressive, yet somehow I got the impression he was hostile, that his question about genetic engineering was outright condemnation. I felt defensive, and I wasn't sure why. Perhaps Mariel could tell us more about his attitude later.

"The suits are for protection," said Nathan calmly. Because we'd already been seen without them he couldn't claim that it was routine, and therefore he had to steer a course much closer to the truth than he would have liked. "We knew that this world had a rich complement of parasitic organisms," he went on, "and when we saw the growth on the skin of the men who came to meet us we feared that it might be one such. We felt it better to be safe until we had talked to you and you had explained it to us."

At least the truth constituted a kind of challenge. The way was clear for the Ego to offer us some kind of explanation.

The man in black didn't hesitate. "The word 'parasite' is wrong," he said. "You do not understand. I cannot attempt to explain at this time. How many people are there aboard your ship?"

"Seven in all," replied Nathan.

"And what, precisely, do you intend to do here?"

"We would like to stay for several months," said Nathan. "Perhaps a year. We would like to examine the colony in detail, in order to prepare a full report. We would like to study its history and its geography, its sociology and its ecology. We would like to examine the people and the land. And, as I have said, we would like to help you in dealing with any difficulties you have encountered in establishing yourselves."

He didn't deny that there were any difficulties. That was odd. Everywhere we went the people denied they had problems—or declared that they didn't want our help in dealing with them. Nobody was ever glad to see us, and the situation suggested that this man was even less pleased than the others. He was treating us with the utmost caution. But he didn't say right out that Arcadia needed no help and that we might as well go right now. He was too cautious even for that.

"It may be good that you should learn about us," he said. "But that is for the Self to decide. What do you think of our city?"

Nathan rode the switchback conversation with ease. Abrupt changes of direction never bothered him.

"It's beautiful," he said. "Why did you take as your model Campanella's description of the City of the Sun?"

"The design was appropriate."

"And are you, then, the metaphysicus—an autocratic high priest?" It was a sharp question. Nathan had apparently decided that what went for the opposition should go for him too.

"Our Nation needs no autocrat," said the man in black, "and God needs no priests." The second sentence, at least, sounded significant.

"So it is just the city walls that echo Campanella," said Nathan. "Not your social philosophy. But why the decorations? Surely this is a somewhat...flamboyant...gesture?"

The Ego sipped patiently at his tea. "The walls communicate," he said. "They contain the knowledge of the Nation. They represent the Nation."

"Chipped stones are not knowledge. They can do no more than symbolize it."

"That is all that is necessary."

I had the feeling that we weren't winning the debate. I had a thousand questions, but I knew how difficult they were to ask. Even with the barrier of scrupulous politeness gone there was no way I was going to find out what I needed to know about the black parasite in conversation.

"What form of government do you have?" asked Nathan. "What is the Self that makes your decisions?"

"It is our collective will," he replied.

"But how do you establish the collective will? By voting? How are decisions actually taken?"

"If you are allowed to remain on this world," replied the Ego, with perfect equanimity, "you will come to understand. And the Self, in its turn, will come to understand you. I do not think that understanding is possible at this time. Are you frightened by what you see in the city?"

It was a very delicate way of putting the issue. Not: *are you frightened by the black markings on our bodies?* but: *are you frightened by what you see in the city?*

"We are disposed to caution," said Nathan, carefully. "We do not yet understand, and thus we are wary. But we are not afraid."

"The people seem strange to you?"

"Of course. But not everything that is strange is implicitly fearful. We have visited several alien worlds. We have seen many things which were strange when we first encountered them."

The Ego rose quickly to his feet then. He had obviously mastered the art of rising from a low cushion. We hadn't, and we had to use our hands to push ourselves up in a somewhat ungainly fashion.

"You must wait in another room now," he said. "We will give you beds. You may sleep while the Self decides whether you will be allowed to stay here. In the morning, you will hear the decision."

"Thank you," said Nathan, with a slight bow. The Ego walked to the door, moving easily and lightly. We followed him. The same man that had brought us was waiting outside, in the corridor, and he led us a few small steps to another door, and let us into one of the rooms at the outer edge of the building. Then he closed the door behind us. I almost expected to hear the sound of a key or a bolt, but the door wasn't equipped for locking.

We heard him move away, and then we were alone.

"Well," said Nathan, "what the hell do you make of this?"

CHAPTER SIX

This room, like the inner chamber, was furnished only with cushions and a single low table, but three of the cushions—positioned against the walls—were huge enough to qualify as beds. The corners of the room were curtained, and behind one I found a bowl of lukewarm water and a toilet seat. The hole seemed bottomless, but there was no offensive smell.

This room had a window, set in a door which gave out onto a balcony, but a thick piece of curtain was tacked over it to prevent a draught. Even so, the room was very cold—had it not been for the suits we would have been less than comfortable. I tested the door to the balcony. It wasn't locked.

Mariel sat down on one of the "beds" before beginning to answer Nathan's question. Nathan and I followed suit.

"In normal circumstances," she said, "people are most readable when they're asking questions and when they're evading them. In the first case, the answers they expect tend to show up in their faces, in the second case, the answers they avoid. That man did nothing but ask and evade questions, but I couldn't pick up a thing. He's like the others—mechanical. It's as if he were an actor reading from a script. Uninvolved. He *didn't* anticipate answers, or let the ones he was hiding materialize unspoken in his mind. It was just as if he weren't a person at all, but an arm or a leg working by habit and reflex. There's an active consciousness somewhere, but it's only a shadow in his facial expressions, in anything I could really feel."

"In other words," said Nathan, "he's being controlled."

"Are you *sure* about this?" I asked her.

"No," she said. "Of course I'm not sure. I'm telling you what impression I get. Even putting it into words distorts it—and maybe I'm choosing all the wrong words. Maybe *control* is a bad one. But I think that he's under some kind of *influence* all right...something which is reducing his independence drastically. His mind is so *ordered*...it *has* become machinelike."

How could I argue? She seemed certain, and she was laying it on the line quite clearly. There seemed to be only one possible interpretation that could be put on the evidence we had.

"It looks bad," I agreed. "What's our next move?"

"It isn't our move at all," said Nathan, dourly. "It's theirs. All the moves are theirs, for the present."

"Do you think they'll tell us to get off their world and never to darken their doorstep again?" asked Mariel.

"I've a feeling," he said, "that there may be worse prospects than that."

"Here we are in the parlor," I said, acidly, "as the fly said nervously to the spider. But they're still thinking about it. They could have grabbed us at any time."

"They're testing us out," said Nathan. "They knew how many of us were coming...so they must have known about the suits. But they prepare tea and dry fruit, to see if politeness is going to make us open up. That was no interrogation we went through...he could have asked a thousand detailed questions if he'd wanted to. The fact that he didn't can only mean one thing."

"He didn't expect to get truthful answers," I supplied.

"They're afraid of us," said Nathan. "They're afraid of the impression that they might have made. They don't want us to go away because they aren't sure they can *afford* to let us get away. On the other hand, do they dare let us stay...if staying means that we get a chance to study this thing and perhaps find a way of destroying it. The thing they *really* want to do is capture the ship...make sure it never leaves. But they know full well that that won't be easy. The purpose of this interview was for the so-called Ego—or whatever's pulling his strings—to find out just how suspicious we are. The simple fact that we have the suits on must have told him more than enough. Our heads are right between the alligator's jaws."

The metaphor was lurid, but I had to admit that it summed up the way I was feeling, too. In the meantime, though, I thought there was still room for caution.

"All this is still speculation," I said. "There's one hell of a lot we don't understand. If the people here are just helpless instruments of the parasite, why the city? Why the walls? And don't forget that we're dreaming up quite some story for this parasite. A hundred years ago it was a simple species parasitizing herbivores of various kinds. Now, we reckon, it's adapted to human hosts, its cells have not only learned to mimic human nervous tissue but to aggregate that tissue in thinking brains and these thinking brains have taken over the thinking brains of their hosts. That's one hell of a story.... It's bordering on the incredible."

"As a story," countered Nathan, "it's impossible. But it's not a story. It's what we see. Even without Mariel's evidence we have a lot to go on. The Ego shows a distinct hostility toward the idea of genetic engineering—sure, it may be some kind of ecological morality, but it looks to me like straightforward anxiety. The Ego makes no decisions of his own—they have to be referred back to something called the Self. Even the nomenclature is significant—the *ego* is only a part of the psyche, the *self* is the whole. As if his mind existed in parallel with another."

"In parallel," I interrupted, "doesn't necessarily mean under control. Maybe the parasite growth has developed its own brain, its own consciousness.... But even that doesn't say that one has to dominate the other. It could be a kind of partnership—a symbiosis. This parasite is considerate, remember.... It goes to extremes to avoid impairing the efficiency of its hosts."

"But there's one other thing he said," Nathan went on. "Maybe the most revealing thing of all. He said: *Our Nation needs no autocrat, and God needs no priests.* Now why doesn't the Nation need an autocrat or God any priests? Maybe because the Nation is ruled from outside and its God is sitting on the back of every single man, woman and child. And I notice that the solicitude of the parasite for its hosts takes some rather strange forms—like the de-sexing of the warrior caste and the civil service, for instance."

"He said other things too," I reminded Nathan. "He said that the Self was a collective will...maybe the collective will of human mind and passenger mind."

"Would you bet your life on that? Or your mind?"

"They're already on the table," I pointed out. "Those are the stakes, whether we like it or not."

The argument wasn't fierce—we were trying to clarify things, not tear out one another's throats. But the room acquired a tense atmosphere anyhow. We were all very much on edge. All frightened, despite what Nathan had told our gracious host.

I opened the door to the balcony and stepped out. I was hoping to be able to look down and see the whole city spread before me, radiating out on all sides. But the innermost wall was too high. All I could see were the shadowed gardens and a few fugitive lights in the buildings within that final wall. The faint sound of the city still told me nothing.

Here we are, I thought, perched on top of an anthill. Strangers in the nest. Prisoners of the warrior caste. The other castes must be different categories of workers. Differentiated by the color of their clothing. But what kind of workers? Slaves? Automata? How many are neutered? After all, it makes sense...just as it makes sense in the anthill. A few drones can supply all the necessary sperm to keep society growing. Of course, you can't have a human queen who lays a thousand eggs a time, so there'd have to be a fairly considerable breeding stock—either a particular caste of women, or all women in a particular age group. Neat, efficient.... Utopian.

A door opened down below, and half a dozen people came out onto the path, and went away in the direction of the gate. They did so silently, with common accord. By the light that spilled out of the door while it was open I saw that they were dressed like the dark man who'd been our guide, in silvery fancy cloth. Others of his kind—perhaps he was with them. Servants, as he'd styled them.

I wondered where they were going. Into the city to conduct a plebiscite, perhaps.

Nathan came out to join me, and saw them walking away into the trees.

"Is it over so soon then?" he asked. "I thought it was scheduled to take all night."

"Maybe it's only just beginning," I said.

"No chance of making a break for it," he mused.

"And if we could?" I said. "If we could all get back to the ship? What then? Take off for Earth and ask them to send out a task force?"

"We can't fight this thing on our own," he said. "Can we?"

"I don't know," I said. "There's far too much I don't know. I don't like to think of running away from this situation without knowing more."

"Knowing a little bit more might cost Earth everything we already know," be reminded me. "We've already been criminally stupid—we should have brought a radio set so we could relay everything to Conrad."

"If we'd only thought," I said, ironically, "we could have left him sealed orders to be opened only in the event of our failure to return. That's what they do in melodramas."

He looked at me soberly. "If this were a melodrama," he said, "then the parasite's strategy would be to take over you and me and Mariel, get us to carry it into the ship, then take over everyone else. Then it would fly the ship back to Earth and begin conquering the entire human race. If this were a melodrama."

"And is it?" I asked him.

He turned and went back inside. I followed, closing the door behind me. Mariel was still sitting on the bed, her back against the wall, watching us closely. She'd heard every word.

"In melodramas," she said, "evil monsters don't spend all

night making decisions. They always know what to do."

She had a point. The Self was deciding. That meant there was some ambivalence in the situation.

I laid myself down on one of the giant cushions, flat on my back. It wasn't very comfortable—certainly not interior sprung. Nathan followed my example, and we all pretended for a few minutes that we were going to sleep. We didn't have to use the toilet—the suits made provision for such problems—and none of us fancied a wash.

"If nothing else," said Nathan, not sounding too happy about it, "this could queer our mission beyond hope of redemption. Unless, somehow, we can pull off a miracle."

What he meant was that our report on this world—if we ever got to make one—was going to put the wind up a lot of people. We'd found colonies on Floria and Wildeblood that were at least semi-successful, and so far we were in a position to make out a moderately good case for the resumption of the space colony program. But if we turned in a story about black spiderweb parasites taking over human beings, robbing men of their manhood and turning the whole colony into a glorified ant hive...prospects wouldn't look so good. In fact, we probably wouldn't have a cat in hell's chance of persuading the UN to persuade the individual nations that putting money into such a scheme would be worthwhile.

"Even for a disaster," said Nathan, rambling on for the sake of talking, "you can work up a pretty good story. You can tell a tale of heroism and struggle against great odds, and you can put in a lot of soul-stirring stuff about conquering the star worlds even in the face of huge odds. But for something like this, you can't do a thing. It makes up its own formula. Pure horror story. Scare sensationalism. Even without the devil's advocate this would be one hell of a voice against us."

"What devil's advocate?" I asked.

"I don't know who it is, of course," said Nathan, "but there must be one. Surely you realized that? This mission makes no pretense to be an unbiased fact-finding mission. I'm here to try and gather ammunition for a war of ideas—to try and give Pietrasante what he needs to remount the colony program. It doesn't make sense that the opposition wouldn't put a man—or woman—in to prepare a different case."

"But how would they get him past Pietrasante?" I asked. The idea really was new to me. I just hadn't ever thought of it before.

"They wouldn't have to," said Nathan. "Pietrasante would be forced to agree. You know how committees work, Alex. Balance and compromise.... Always have the cake and eat it too.... Never decide one way or the other if you can have both. He knows there's a member of the opposition aboard, but to him that's a fairly ordinary fact of life."

"Who is it?" I asked.

"I don't know," he said. "And I don't suppose Mariel's telling."

You can't keep secrets from a mind-reader. You just have to rely on the mind-reader to keep them for you. And, of course, she would. No mind-reader could possibly get along in life without a lot of discretion. The *Daedalus* was a smooth-running ship now—we'd all got used to having Mariel aboard. But that smooth running was dependent on Mariel's integrity. If we so much as suspected that anything she inadvertently picked up from any of us might become common property....

I didn't insult her by asking her who the devil's advocate was. Now I looked at the situation coldly, it didn't really matter. It made no difference at all.

Somewhere inside me, I felt the fear that had gripped me— the fear of the parasite, that is—ebbing slightly as the new anxiety arose. Even if we got away...the mission was dead. What we'd already accomplished was real enough, but the greater purpose...the thing that really *mattered,* at least to me, was lost.

Barring miracles.

I closed my eyes deliberately, trying to pretend even to myself that sleep might be possible. But I knew that even if I could sleep I wouldn't have pleasant dreams.

CHAPTER SEVEN

We didn't see or hear the Servants returning to the pyramid, but when we were finally ushered downstairs again there were eight of them waiting in the large hall. The Ego was there, too. It was official pronouncement time.

I had a lump in my throat as I waited for him to begin his speech.

It cleared rapidly, and I felt a tide of relief unexpected in its intensity, before he was halfway through. It returned, alas, before he finished.

"It has been decided," he said, "that you may stay here. We think it is a good thing that you should study us and try to understand the way that we live. We doubt that there is any help that you can offer us, but if we should discover grounds for cooperation then we will be pleased to accept your assistance.

"There are, however, certain conditions which we must attach to this decision. We feel that it is vital for both the Nation and yourselves that the understanding which you gain of what has happened and is happening on Arcadia should be complete and accurate. We offer you twenty days to make preliminary observations, but in doing so you must not harm any creature which is augmented by the black companion which you have erroneously called a parasite. Nor may you conduct experiments upon any companion cells.

"At the end of twenty days one of your number must himself—or herself—accept a companion. Only by experience is understanding genuinely possible.

"The association need only be temporary if that is your wish. That is the judgment of the Self. Do you agree?"

I was left a little breathless, but Nathan didn't so much as hesitate. "We too are subject to a collective will," he said. "We three cannot decide here and now. We must return to the ship to confer with the others."

"A Servant will escort you," said the Ego, with perfect equanimity. "When may we expect your decision?"

"This evening," said Nathan, promptly.

The changes of pace had left me behind a little, but as we mounted up—one beast each, this time—at the spot where we had dismounted the night before, I began to review the situation. We were being given the opportunity to run, if we wanted to. We could take our jumped conclusions back to Earth. But we were also being tempted to stay, with twenty clear days before the crunch. If they were prepared to offer us that much rope, could they possibly be the monsters that our fears had painted them? Or were they simply trying to give us the opportunity to hang ourselves?

We rode downhill with the early morning traffic. It was hardly any more crowded than the previous evening, but it was daylight now, and the white and yellow tunics seemed very bright. There were more ox-carts ahead of us and behind us, some empty but some carrying groups of laborers with agricultural tools. The tools were mostly wooden—only a few had metal blades and tines.

Whether it was because we were going downhill or because the tempo of the beasts' movements had been deliberately stepped up I'm not sure, but it didn't take us long to get out of the city. I didn't get much of a view of the wondrous walls because I had to look back over my shoulder to see the pictographs after we had passed through each gate.

Once outside the city the oxen were encouraged into a gait which might have been their version of a trot, and we covered the country rather more efficiently than we had previously done. Even so, I had no doubt that the animals could have gone a great deal faster had they been encouraged. I was impressed by their docility and their cooperativeness, but somewhat worried about the means by which this had been achieved. To what extent was the parasite modifying their behavior? And to what extent was the "companion" riding the neck of my mount in touch with—and possibly governed by—other companions of other hosts? It was going to be difficult to find out if both the parasite and its hosts were taboo.

The dark man escorted us patiently. He didn't say anything, and Nathan didn't try to ask him any questions. This may have been because his mind was on getting back to the ship and nothing else, or it may have been that he couldn't guide his mount close enough to the dark man's to make striking up a conversation feasible.

When we got back Karen, Conrad and Linda were all asleep. They hadn't had our problems, despite the fact that they could have had the grace to worry themselves sleepless over our fate. We didn't wake them immediately, but got some tubes of lique-fied food to squeeze through the filters. Mariel was lucky—after external decontamination she could jettison her suit and get some real food.

I let Nathan tell the story to the others. He gave a blow-by-blow account, not too heavily biased by commentary and infer-ence.

He finished up by saying: "They obviously aren't scared of us. They're giving us the chance to run despite the fact that they must have a clear idea of how this situation looks to us. They're asking for a chance to explain...and I'm not quite sure whether 'they' is the people or the things on their backs. Either way, maybe we owe it to them. We need to know more. We have to stay...at least for twenty days."

"And then?" said Conrad.

I looked round to see if anyone wanted to argue that we should leave right away. Nobody did.

"That depends what we find out in the meantime," I said.

"You'd seriously consider exposing one of us to infection by this thing?" asked Linda.

"Why not?" I replied. "We can deal with the infection if need be. And their top man is right. The only way we're likely to be able to understand, fully and accurately, what has happened here, is to experience it."

"You're volunteering, I hope?" said Linda.

"Maybe," I said, refusing to be backed off. "If the situation seems right, maybe I will."

"You're going too fast, Alex," Nathan intervened. "Let's not start squabbling over the short straw until the occasion presents itself. We have something much more important to decide."

"But surely we stay," I said. "That's already settled."

"Not that," he said. "What we have to talk about now is how we can possibly go about trying to find out what we want to know. Put crudely, the question is: are we dealing with alien minds manipulating human bodies, or human minds that have been passively modified, or human minds in association with alien minds, or what? I'm not asking for guesses as to which one.... I'm asking how we could possibly find out. How do we test?"

There was a pensive silence. This was, of course, the crucial question. How do you tell a puppet from a free agent? How do you tell passive modification from active control?

"We're not allowed to analyze any of the parasite material?" said Linda, asking for confirmation.

"Nor harm any host," I added.

"In that case," said Conrad, "all we have is indirect measurement and asking questions. Could we rig up something like an encephalograph to sound out electrical activity in the external bulk of the parasite?"

I shrugged. "Suppose it is pseudo-nervous tissue...and electrically active. That won't tell us whether it's independent, let alone sentient."

"In that case," said Conrad, shrugging in his turn, "all we have is guesswork...unless we're prepared to believe what they tell us."

"There must be *some* way," said Nathan.

I thought hard. No startling inspiration materialized.

"Without being able to experiment directly...," I said, hesitantly, "...then I think Conrad's right. We have to rely on question-and-answer. And our lie detector is, for once, just as likely to be fooled as we are."

"Perhaps their concessions aren't quite so generous," said Conrad. "They're giving us time...but they're also giving themselves time. They know we'll stay for the twenty days—and that could give them twenty days to work out a method of infiltrating the ship, if that's their aim."

Nathan scowled as he tried to concentrate on the intricacies of the situation. "It could be," he said, "that letting the three of us come back here was no more than a shrewd ploy. If they'd held on to us Pete would have lifted the ship—eventually—and they'd have shown their hand for no real gain. This way, they could be giving themselves leeway to mount something rather more ambitious."

I didn't like the direction the conversation was taking. Nathan had one hell of a suspicious mind. But under the circumstances, what other way was there for it to go? While we didn't know what was what and couldn't find out we had to guard against all eventualities. We had to assume that the worst was at least possible, and work out a strategy to cope with it.

"How much information on this stuff is in the survey report, Alex?" asked Nathan. "Assuming, that is, that you've picked out the right candidate."

"I told you. Standard data."

"What I mean is: is there enough data for us to begin work on preparing something to attack it. Not necessarily a virus...a specific poison."

I shook my head. "I can tell you about poisons that will destroy just about any kind of living tissue," I said. "But to identify something that will attack this stuff specifically without a living specimen to work with is impossible. It would *have* to be genetically specific, remember.... This stuff can mimic the cells of its hosts well enough to avoid any ordinary antibiotic. And while we're on the subject there's one other thing that you ought to bear in mind."

"What's that?"

"Don't bank on our being able to wipe this thing out, even if things do go entirely our way. With a living specimen to work on and the resources of the lab I could devise a way to protect us. But for the people in the city it's already too late. Quite apart from the psychological dependency—however great or small that may be—there's the fact that the parasite probably has extensive ramifications inside the body. If we find something that kills parasite cells selectively those people will wake up one morning to find that there's the detritus of millions of dead cells washing about in their system. Their physiological resources wouldn't be up to the job of cleaning them out. The breakdown products would be toxic—would poison the host system. The only way those people are going to be freed from parasitism is if the parasite can be persuaded to withdraw an inch at a time. I don't see how we'd arrange that."

"There's one way we could attack the problem," said Conrad, quickly. "If we found the means and the opportunity."

"Which is?" asked Nathan.

"We'd have to find an agent—an innovative gene—that wouldn't actively destroy the parasite but would immunize against initial infection. If we could attach it to a carrier virus and make it endemic in the population it would protect newborn children against the possibility of parasitism."

"You can do that?" said Nathan, checking with me.

"We *might* be able to," I agreed. "If we had time—a lot more than twenty days. And if we had living cells to work with. And if we had a little luck riding with us. But before there's any question of our being able to mount such a project there's the problem of getting the people to cooperate, knowingly or not. While they stick to their conditions we have no chance...and there is, of course, one more unknown factor, which is the resources of the parasite. We may be the genetic engineers but organisms have their own way of coping with difficulties. If each of these black things were an organism, it would be different, but they're not. Each one is a colony of millions of organisms, with a generation time probably measurable in hours. That's quite some reservoir of potential for change...for extreme adaptability. We already know that each cell has tremendous versatility. Most of the problems we try to overcome with the aid of our little laboratory are easy. This one might fight back. And it might win. It may be able to develop its own immunity to our immunizing agent just as fast as we can develop it in the lab. Maybe faster."

I looked at Conrad for support.

He nodded. "All that's true," he said. "Nature's provided this thing with all the resources that technology's given us. It may conduct its evolutionary experiments without much planning, but it has the equipment to get there anyhow—the opportunity to mount so many trials that errors don't matter."

"If this stuff is as versatile as all that and twice as clever," said Karen, "how come we're so confident we can defend ourselves against it?"

"Its resources are purely reactive," I said. "We have to set it the problem before it gets to solve it. It can't take the offensive. At least, not unless it's...." I let the sentence hang, realizing the awful possibility.

"Not unless it's sentient," Conrad finished for me.

"But that's exactly what we don't know," said Nathan.

"True," I admitted. "But twenty days is only twenty days.... God Almighty would be pushed to create something capable of breaching the ship and the suits in that time."

"Not if the rumors about his strenuous working week are true," said Karen, sarcastically. "In addition to which, it may be that a god—though maybe not an almighty one—is what we're facing. Nathan quoted something their top man said which suggests that the colonists just might regard this thing as a god."

"That, at least, we can investigate," I said. "We're entitled to ask questions about their beliefs, religious and otherwise. In fact it may be that questions about their beliefs are the only ones that are going to reveal anything significant. If they do believe in an active divine force that might be testimony to the existence of an independent sentience in the parasitic communities."

"On the other hand," said Nathan, dryly, "it might not. Plenty of people have held similar beliefs without being dominated by parasites. And on the other hand, even if they don't believe in any independent active force, that wouldn't prove that there isn't one."

I shrugged my shoulders. "Just an idea," I said. "At least that's one area where you're less likely to encounter straightforward lies."

He shook his head, unconvinced. He was now in a situation where he was prepared to doubt any and all evidence. We might be faced with a situation where any and all evidence was dubious, so perhaps it was fair enough. But once you get into such a morass of doubt how do you ever get out? How can you?

"Should we reconsider our decision?" said Pete, carefully. "If we not only don't know where we are but don't know any way that we can get anywhere at all, what's the point in staying? Maybe we should duck the risks and go home...pass the buck back to the UN."

"And what would *they* do?" I inquired.

"One of two things," said Nathan. "Forget the whole thing. Or send a bomb to cancel the problem out of existence. And either way...."

"Our mission would be a bust. The devil's advocate is left with a walkover."

"Probably."

I looked round the table. "I say we stay," I said. "I say we have to be prepared to have a go at this thing ourselves. It may be impossible, but it may not. Either way, we must try. Even if there's a risk."

"I'm with Alex," said Nathan. "Anyone else?"

"We've nothing to run away from yet but a complicated argument," said Conrad.

"We have to *try*," said Mariel.

That was a majority. If any of the others had seriously considered being a dissenting voice they shelved their plans now. Karen and Linda just nodded, and Pete said: "That's okay."

"Then let's get to work," said Nathan. "Let's get what we can before the first deadline. *But be careful.*"

The mood which dominated the commencement of work was not one of overwhelming self-confidence.

CHAPTER EIGHT

With such a short time to go before the big hurdle had to be jumped (or refused) we had to set to work with determination, and perhaps even a hint of desperation. Conrad and Linda began in the fields, assessing the agricultural status of the colony, but moved on as soon as they had collected basic data and sufficient specimens for later scrutinization into the city, where they began to investigate diet, hygiene and health. They found the citizens cooperative but not talkative. They were allowed to take blood samples but there was always a Servant in attendance to make sure that the parasite cells weren't touched. These data were given priority in analysis.

The rest of us also found that we were shadowed just about everywhere that we went by helpful but suspicious Servants. We'd lived with exactly the same problem during our early days on Wildeblood, and we were used to it—but that didn't make it any less of an imposition. Nathan and Mariel went straight into the city with all kinds of recording apparatus—film and tape. It took them only a couple of days to get a basic record of the situation in glorious Technicolor, and Mariel was left to sort through the film in search of anything helpful while Nathan carried on the interrogation work he'd already begun. The most unenviable part of Mariel's task was the sorting, classification and filing of the pictographs, but this, too, was given a low priority as too time-consuming for immediate attention. Nathan, of course, asked for help in translating—or perhaps interpreting would be a better word—the pictographs, and this was readily granted. It turned out, however, that anyone he stopped in the street could tell him the meaning of any pictograph. He spent a whole day trying to find the limits of ignorance, and was finally forced to the conclusion, incredibly enough, that everyone in the city really did know the meaning of every single pictograph. Most of the tiles were single words, but some were whole sentences.

"It's just not possible," he told me. "A lot of the pictures are more-or-less recognizable images. A lot of the ones that stand for sentences are compounded from simpler ones—and though I haven't seen more than a tiny fraction I presume that's generally true. But it gives every man, woman and child in the city—no matter what caste they belong to—a vocabulary of more than a million units. I don't know how long it takes the small children to learn it but I couldn't even catch a ten-year-old admitting he didn't know. Maybe some of them were lying, but every time I asked for confirmation I got it. It is just *not* possible."

I had to agree with him.

I had a certain allocation of purely routine work to do as well, of course—several hours every day had to be given to sample collecting and measurement. We were determined that if we had to go home after twenty days we'd have plundered the city of every datum that was available at the surface, to give ourselves at least a chance of drawing more accurate conclusions about what might lie under the surface. But I also involved myself in the confrontation merry-go-round of questions and answers.

I found—as did the others—that in matters of information the people were quite reliable. And they did display the most astonishing range of knowledge. Even children could immediately find the name of any plant or animal or geographical feature. The only limitation I could find even in the knowledge of the children was that it was unrefined—a great many objects might be assigned to one general category. As they got older, they learned to subdivide the categories more and more precisely.

Against this astonishing range of knowledge that was carried in every head had to be set certain curious anomalies. Everyone in the city could read the pictographs, but that was all there was to be read. Nothing else existed. The data bank brought out from Earth had been deliberately destroyed. Nor did the people of the city go in for painting. Either something was chipped into the stone adorning the city walls or it had no existence independent of the minds of the people. The only arts which they had apart from the stone masonry were the performing arts—drama, music, dance. Nothing was ever written down. But they were interested in growing things. Many of the houses that I visited—little, square cubicles with only curtains separating different "rooms"—contained potted plants.

All this, however, was peripheral to our main concern. And when we got beyond mere matters of information, we found ourselves on much trickier ground in asking our questions. Questions, regarding the parasite and matters of belief were evaded quite casually, or answered by rote. Questions about the decision-making process were met with the blanket answer: "The Self decides." "What is the Self?" conjured forth the reply: "The Self is the collective will of the Nation." More detailed questions ("How does the Self decide?" "What actually *happens* when decisions are made?") called forth blank stares or statements to the effect that: "You do not understand." That was true. We didn't. Persistence drew forth the promise that one day we *would* understand...the day in question being day twenty-one.

Questions relating to religion met a similar defensive wall without any hint of a breach. Everyone in the city believed in God—an apparently unshakable monotheistic belief. But they had no priests, no churches, no sacred writings. There was a pictograph representing the concept of God, and Nathan managed to identify a couple more which related to matters of divine nature. No doubt there were more—and no doubt given time we could extract from the wisdom of the walls all that the people of the city thought it necessary to say about God. But we didn't have time to learn the meanings of millions of tiles. We needed more direct access to the information, and we couldn't get it. All we could find out was that they all *knew* that God existed, and that was enough for them.

"If our questions are being deliberately stonewalled," I told Nathan, after a couple of days of the run-around, "then it's the best job I've ever seen. Wherever we turn we get the same barrier, the same formulae. If they're deliberately holding back the whole truth from us then every single person in the city is in on the conspiracy, including children. It's the most perfect collusion I've ever encountered. They all know exactly how much to say, to the very letter. Either this really is the limit of their own concern with the matter, or something very strange is happening here."

"They could be programmed," he said. "Every one primed by the puppeteers."

"Or they could be telepathic," I said. "With everyone of them having access to the same pool of information and the same set of stalling strategies."

"Or both," he added.

"Only they don't appear to communicate with one another telepathically," I said. "They use language, like you and me. And if they're programmed it's an ultra-complete and perfect job. They still seem very human to me, despite what Mariel says."

"Appearances," he declared, "can be deceptive."

And that statement, of course, represented the farthest shore of knowledge. Beyond it there was only a limitless ocean of uncertainty.

Such is life.

We did manage to find out that their caste system wasn't hierarchical, unless you counted the Servants and the Ego as "superior." Even that was in doubt. They had special functions, to be sure—functions that didn't involve getting their hands dirty—but I never once saw a Servant handing out orders or supervising work. If they had authority they didn't use it conspicuously. No one, so far as we could tell, had any special privileges attached to his status or his work. The City of the Sun seemed to go in very seriously for Utopian egalitarianism. Everyone took the role allotted to him by the Self...but all our attempts to find out how that allotment was worked came to nothing, lost in the maze of evasions which confounded all our efforts in this area.

We discovered also that the colony had little interest in technological development. They quarried stone but did not mine metal. The gas that lit the lamps illuminating the walls was generated from the city's wastes and from certain species of seaweed collected along the shore. The oil they used also came from seaweed harvested from the shallow waters that stretched for miles from the river's mouth. All the metal they used—for their tools, for their chisels, for their gas plant and for a hundred other minor purposes—had originally come from the ships that had brought the colony here in the first place. We expressed some surprise at this discovery, asking whether the city wouldn't have to develop its own supply eventually, but they didn't have any answer. They didn't seem very interested in the future.... They had nothing to say about any kind of long-term plan. Nor, for that matter, did they have much interest in the past. We tried to ask searching questions about how and when the present state of affairs had arisen, but they offered no answers. If they had any memory of a time before the parasite, they were keeping it a secret. The one thing they did tell us was where the ships had actually come down.

This, in the absence of any written record of events in the colony or any verbal account of the early days, seemed to me to be a valuable datum. The ships had all come down within a few miles of one another, but some distance inland. Whatever remained of the nearest one was a full day's ride to the northwest, a long way up the river valley. I suggested to Nathan that one of us, at least, should go up there to investigate. The relic might tell us nothing...but there just might be something of significance to be found there. Nathan didn't want to waste two days—one riding out, one coming back—in the present circumstances, with time so limited, but I pointed out that with the information blockade so firm anything we might find out by inference from objective evidence was worth going after. In the end, he agreed to my going. I showed a measure of compromise by agreeing to go alone.

I wasn't unduly surprised that when I explained to the dark man that I wanted to borrow one of the oxen to ride out into the wilderness he promptly volunteered to go with me. Partly, I thought, it was because he wanted to keep an eye on me...but I think he also wanted to keep an eye on the ox. If I were to ride away on a beast that carried the parasite without anyone to see what I was doing....

They seemed very keen to make sure that the conditions we had agreed to were obeyed. They were particularly careful to make sure that none of the black cells were appropriated for study.

I was slightly more surprised when the Servant turned up with four archers. We hadn't seen much of the archers since our first trip to the city—they'd been discreetly confined to their inner circle barracks. When I asked the Servant what they were needed for, he simply said: "It is dangerous."

"What kind of danger?" I asked.

"Carnivores," he replied.

The river valley supported large herds of the yak-deer, and various smaller herbivorous species ranging in size from mice to sheep. There were various carnivores that preyed on them, but the only ones likely to be dangerous to a mounted man were dog-like creatures carelessly labelled "wolves" which hunted in packs.

"They attack men?" I asked.

"Yes," he replied. "Sometimes it is still necessary to take carts overland to strip metal from the remains of the ships. When we make camp at night, the carnivores come. And if there is injury—the smell of blood on the wind will bring them."

"That's why you have archers? To defend caravans against carnivores?"

"And to defend the beasts in the fields," he confirmed.

"The beasts? Or their companions?"

His black eyes met mine unwaveringly. "Beast and companion are one," he said.

The parasite infested only herbivorous species. No carnivore could have a companion. The people of the city were all vegetarians, although they ate fish and drank milk. They wouldn't have dreamed of eating any creature that might carry the parasite—or was potentially capable of so doing—and they expressed distaste at the prospect of eating carnivore meat as well, lest they should be consuming second-hand the flesh of a host creature.

Our ill-assorted party set out in the early hours of the morning—a while before dawn—and followed the river northward. For the first time the all-purpose yak-deer showed me what they could do in terms of speed. I was pleasantly surprised, not so much by the pace, but by the fact that even when they were going at a steady trot they were quite stable. I had anticipated an extremely uncomfortable ride, and expected to pay with soreness for my two-day jaunt into the wilderness, but it wasn't that bad.

The Servant led the way, while the archers grouped themselves around me like a guard of honor. I didn't find it a very satisfactory arrangement, and tried to match strides with the dark man so that conversation would be possible. My mount responded well enough to my urging, but the Servant—without being too obvious about it—kept trying to drift away to a discreet distance. I persisted until he would have had to make it obvious that he was deliberately avoiding me, and finally he capitulated.

"This is good land," I said. "Most colonies would have spread out to occupy it—the people coming out from Earth appreciate the space, the room to expand. Why do you stay huddled together in the city, cultivating just enough land to support you?"

"We are one Nation," he replied. "We live together."

"Staying in one place makes you vulnerable to disaster," I pointed out. "One bad winter—one blight—any kind of disaster—would have you in serious trouble."

"We have enough for our needs," he said. "There is always more food in the sea."

"And what happens as your population expands?" I asked. "Do you keep adding walls to the city, and extending the ring of cultivated land around it? You can't do that forever."

"The Self will decide," he assured me.

I had no doubt of it. It would decide to limit population, one way or another. Or it would decide that another city should be built, and another, and another....

But he wasn't interested. He just knew that when the question arose it would be answered. I couldn't understand that lack of interest in future possibilities. How was he motivated if not by anticipation of some kind or another? But his life promised him no rewards that I could understand. He had his role to play and he fulfilled it scrupulously. I was tempted to ask him what his ambitions were, what were his goals in life, but I knew the answer I would get. A blank stare, insulting in its demonstration of lack of comprehension.

One of us is crazy, I thought, and I wish I was sure it isn't me.

The oldest objection to Utopian schemes is that they offer no one the incentive to work. No one depends upon his own efforts, but only on the efforts of the community as a whole. No one does anything for himself, but only for the community as a whole. Cynics say that Utopia can't work. I agreed with them. Ants and bees can do it, but their communities have but a single mind—the collective identity of the hive.

Much of what we had seen here on Arcadia suggested that the people had achieved a similar kind of collective identity—their city and their life were very hive-like. But it was difficult to see how association with the parasite had done that to them—or *for* them. Even if companionship was the biggest kick in the world...even if parasite cells mimicking brain cells gave the host brain new potential and new powers...it was difficult to see how. Unless they were genuinely telepathic. I kept coming back to that possibility. They couldn't read our minds—that was for sure. And Mariel couldn't read theirs. I didn't believe that they could read each other's thoughts, either. Yet they had this extremely strong sense of social unity, an inordinately powerful empathy not with one another but each with the whole.

And they all knew that God existed. They *knew* it, beyond all question. Could that knowledge, I wondered, have its source in the same empathic experience?

"What happens," I asked him, "to people who die?"

His face had relaxed slightly during the silence. Now I saw muscles suddenly tighten. His face was set hard. I knew I was close to the area that the Self had designated as forbidden—the knowledge that was being held back from us until we volunteered for the proper route to understanding.

"Their bodies are destroyed," he said.

"In the gas plant?" I asked. "With the shit and the seaweed?"

"Yes," he replied.

It didn't seem to show much respect. It was logical...perhaps a little too logical. But that wasn't the key issue. What I really wanted to know was.... "And what happens to the companion?"

His face was already set hard, and not a muscle flickered now.

"The companion does not die," he said. Which was true enough. Communalities never die. Individual cells die, but their death doesn't affect the whole in the way that the wearing out of cells affects intricately structured organisms.

"So what happens to it? Does it pull up its roots and wait to be transplanted to a new host?"

"I cannot answer that question," he said. At least it was an unequivocal declaration. *This* is where the barrier comes down. *Here* are the secrets that we're hiding from you for the duration of our twenty-day guessing game.

"And what about the soul of the dead man?" I went on. "Does it get to heaven via the gas generator? Does it rise from the mess to meet its maker?"

The sarcasm, of course, was wasted—and also a little uncalled-for.

"The soul," he replied, "is not changed by death. It is as it always was, in and of the Self."

There, again, was the mentality of the hive. The individual is only a part of the whole. The life and mind of the whole is unaffected by the death of the individual. The individual has been a *part* of the whole, but once dead he is nothing, and the whole is the same. Why should they respect their dead? What do I do with the detritus of a haircut, or with fingernail parings? What do I care about the skin cells that are sloughed off every day? They have been part of me, they are no longer. I am unaltered. But those cells, never had any kind of individual existence. If I were a sentience based in a communal pseudo-organism, would I think the same way? And if I were part of a human society that had somehow acquired the *mentality* of a communal pseudo-organism, could I then think of my own life in the same terms that I thought of the life of those nail parings or skin cells?

Maybe.

But I still couldn't fathom out exactly what might be happening here...what kind of relationship existed between the Arcadians and their parasites. It might be a wonderful partnership, with the black cells giving all kinds of benefits in return for the nutrients they took from their hosts—better control of body and mind, perhaps protection against disease if the parasite's defensive resources were added to the host body's. On the other hand, it might be total control of victim by predator—all the same benefits, but worked exclusively by and for the dendrites and their purely hypothetical independent sentiences generated in plagiarized brains.

Such sentiences, if they did exist, would have some big advantages over their original models. Versatility. And immortality. And the only limitation on their potential and their intelligence would be how big they could grow. How much black parasite tissue could each human support? What kind of extra biomass could the human appetite sustain in addition to its own. I thought back to Earth. I had seen some very big appetites—and I had seen people carrying an awful lot of excess biomass superfluous to—and even endangering—their own requirements.

Even if it's true, I thought, it could be worse. Suppose something like this had evolved on Floria, where everything grows to giant size....

The hills on the west side of the river drew back toward the horizon as we rode, and there was soon a large, flat plain extending away to our left. On the far bank we could still see the moorland beyond the river valley, but the sky was gray and overcast, and the hilltops were blurred by the gloomy cloud.

The vegetation was strangely patchy, dark and light shades of green contrasting to make a kind of mosaic. Where there were trees they tended to grow in small clumps—there were one or two small woods but no forests. We crossed a number of small streams and gullies which brought water from the farther reaches of the river basin. The river itself was wide here and moved slowly in its course.

While we stayed close to the river bank we saw plenty of wildlife. I saw several herds of large herbivores—some the same species as the beasts we were riding. We passed among one herd that had come to the river to drink. They showed no sign of fear. I was interested to note that about half the animals had black dendrites visible beneath the shaggy fur. It was possible that some of the other animals were invisibly infected, but I passed close enough to two to be sure that there were no black lines masked by their fur.

The heath was liberally scattered with burrows that belonged to smaller mammals, and we often saw groups of these feeding in clumps of tall plants, standing on their hind legs and balancing with their tails in order to reach the growing shoots. These creatures were so common that they had to be a major force in maintaining the rather bleak ecological equilibrium in the river valley, stopping the invasion of shrubs and young trees that might take the land toward a forest climax community.

Twice I saw predators attack the groups while they fed—both times successfully—but these carnivores were as small as their victims: long, lean animals like weasels. There was nothing that looked like a wolf—or even a fox.

There were no obvious signs to say that humans had ever passed this way before. I judged that the expeditions to recover metal and plastic from the ships must be few and far between nowadays, and there was nothing else to draw the people of the city out this way. The stone that they used in the city came from quarries and cliff faces along the coastline and in the hills to the northeast of the city, on the far side of the river valley. The stone was transported on barges along the coast and up the river.

As we passed within sight of one of the herds of yak-deer, I steered my way to the side of the Servant again, and said: "If wolves were to appear now, harrying that herd, what would you do?"

"The archers would kill the wolves," he replied.

"And if the pack turned to run—would you pursue them?"

"No."

"Why not? They'd only return once you had gone, or find another herd. You couldn't cheat them of their prey forever."

"We cannot prevent every act of slaughter that occurs in the wilderness," he said, blandly. "If we are nearby, then it is right that we should intervene. But we cannot systematically exterminate the carnivore species."

"Yet," I said.

He didn't reply.

I prompted him. "There may come a time when you have the manpower and the time...maybe not to free the whole world of carnivores, but at least to liberate a lot of herds in these lands. Isn't that a reason for you to expand out here?"

"That," he stated, "is for the Self to decide."

"But it wouldn't be against the Self's principles to mount such a pogrom, would it? If it were possible to exterminate the carnivore populations, drive their species into extinction, you'd do it, wouldn't you?"

"They are carnivores," he replied.

He didn't have the spirit of a true conservationist. His idea of morality—the Self's morality—didn't extend to carnivores.

I wondered whether he knew that when given the opportunity I was a bit of a carnivore myself. I supposed that he did—these people hadn't forgotten all that their ancestors had known on Earth, merely shelved it within their minds and discarded some of what they considered to be the dross. But I, at least, was a redeemable carnivore. If pushed, I could live on a vegetarian diet plus fish, just as they did.

"Some of these animals out here don't have companions," I observed. "Are they immune? Is there some kind of natural check on the spread of the parasite in the wild?"

I didn't really expect much of an answer to that. I knew he wasn't going to tell me anything he might know about immunity. But what he did say was very strange.

He said: "Nothing here is shaped by the Self."

I had to think about that for a moment or two, and he tried to generate some distance between us by urging his mount to the left. I shoved mine in the same direction.

"Are you saying that even the parasitized beasts out here are different in some way from these domesticated ones?" I asked. "Do you mean to say that you also count the beasts of burden in your idea of the Nation's Self?"

"We are one Nation," he replied. It wasn't exactly a flat *yes*, but it wasn't a flat *no*. And surely, if I was wrong, a flat *no* would have served.

Votes for oxen, I thought. *And why the hell not? They pull the ploughs and the carts.*

But oxen were stupid. If ox plus companion added up to something semi-intelligent, the extra contribution could only come from the black dendrite. But how? If the wild oxen out here, parasitized or not, were excluded, what was different about the domestic oxen.

Human hosts die, I thought. *Dendrites don't.*

I looked down at the neck of my trusty steed, wondering if the network of thin black lines might once have been the Servant's Uncle Harry. Or Uncle Harry's companion, to be strictly accurate. If it was, it had lost an awful lot of weight...

unless the internal ramifications of the ox-dendrites were much more extensive than the internal ramifications of the man-parasites....

It was all pure speculation. There was so much speculation. If only one small piece would fall into place perhaps we could sort out the truth from its welter of concealing illusions, and everything would come together. Just one small extra factor... the one that the people of the City of the Sun were so determined to hide from us until the day when they could offer us understanding.... Until the day when understanding might come far too late, if our worst fears were halfway justified.

The Servant had moved away again.

Gentle rain began to fall from above. It didn't bother me—I was dressed for it. It didn't seem to bother the Servant or our cohort of guards, either. The naked archers seemed quite oblivious to wind and water. Whether this was because the parasite enhanced their temperature regulation or whether they were just stoical there was no way to tell. Raindrops settling on the visor blurred my vision, and I wiped them away with my hand. A couple soaked into the leaf-filter and I sucked them through. It took a lot of sucking for a very small payoff.

Which seemed to symbolize our present situation as regarded coming to terms with Arcadia's colony.

CHAPTER NINE

As the day wore on the country seemed to get wilder. The rain never came down really hard but it was steady, and the clouds from which it came seemed to sink toward the earth while the invisible sun sank toward the western horizon. My guard of honor rode on, so steadfastly and uncomplainingly that I felt like apologizing to them for dragging them out on such a day. But there was nothing to say and nothing to see, and I whiled away the hours looking forward to our arrival in the hope that the stripped-down body of the ship might still offer some shelter.

We reached the target with a couple of hours to spare before dark. There wasn't a lot left of what had once been a gigantic machine—a veritable space whale. She'd been built on the moon and then lifted into Earth orbit (gravity was no object so far as her rule-bending drive unit was concerned, but air was— she was built to travel through atmosphere exactly once, on the way down). Her outer hull and most of the bulkheads had been plundered and cannibalized—it was all usable stuff. Everything that could be torn off or ripped out had been. What was left behind was the metal that was impossible to remove—the basic skeleton of the ship and much of the drive unit, plus lots of garbage left over from previous raids. The ground was littered with silica chips and plastic debris too small to improvise into anything useful.

We took shelter near the drive unit, where there was a ridge of structural material—more of a ledge than a roof, but enough to keep the rain off. Two of the archers went out into the gray murk—to collect wood, the Servant solemnly informed me.

"It'll be too wet to burn," I told him.

He didn't deign to answer. He burrowed around in the rain-shadow of the drive unit, and the other archers investigated all the other sheltered cracks and corners, and they assembled a reasonable pile of dead leaves, twigs, tubers and the like that weren't quite dry, but on the other hand weren't exactly soaking. One of the archers reached into the quiver where he carried his arrows and produced a block of some waxy substance. He squeezed it between his fingers and spread the detritus around the pile of rubbish, putting the remainder of the block back into the quiver. He then produced a spark-making device along the lines of a tinderbox and ignited the wax. It flared up, lit the pile of rubbish, and soon burned healthily enough for the damp wood brought back by the foragers to be introduced piece by piece without mishap. It would need constant attention to keep it in, but it was shielded from the rain.

"I thought you people didn't bother so much about keeping warm," I said.

"The night will be cold," said the dark man, affably. "The fire will help to keep us dry. And it will discourage predators. You still have an hour before dark. This is what you came out here to see. Look around."

I took the hint. I was dry anyhow. And I had come to see whatever there was to be seen. Somehow, in the rain it didn't seem like such a good idea. What could picking over the bones of an old spaceship tell me?

There were birds nesting in the articulations of many of the metal limbs. There were a lot of droppings scattered on the ground, suggesting that our arrival had disturbed quite a crowd of small mammals. I searched assiduously for anything that might offer some insight into the years during which the ship had been stripped—a piece of imperishable plastic with something written on it...even graffiti on the skeletal struts. As I looked and didn't find anything I began to feel a little stupid.

But I had to keep looking for one small piece of evidence that might reveal the fact that I was trying to discover: whether the people in the city were, in fact, all the people living on Arcadia. If there were other men here—men without black spider web companions—they, too, must come here to plunder what they could from the wreckage.

I wanted to think that they might exist. Since I had seen the herds earlier in the day, where parasitized beasts mingled with unparasitized beasts, I had—rightly or wrongly—been encouraged to hope. But I needed something else that could ignite that hope into a real possibility. I needed a *sign*. I didn't really know what kind of sign I was looking for, but I was damned if I was going to miss it for want of looking.

But night fell, and I had nothing.

I returned to the shelter and the fire, my plastic outer skin running with tiny rivulets of rainwater.

"You found nothing," said the Servant.

"I found nothing," I confirmed.

"We will go back in the morning."

I gave him a dirty look, but he didn't appreciate it. All expressions came alike to him.

"We'll see how things look in the morning," I replied.

He didn't ask me what I was looking for. Perhaps he thought he knew. Or perhaps he thought I didn't.

They had brought food with them, in packs slung across the hindquarters of the oxen. I'd brought my own rations, properly sterilized and liquefied, in containers that looked like big tooth-paste tubes. They brewed up some of their insipid tea using rainwater, and offered me a bowl. I took it, just to be sociable.

They had no sleeping bags, and were content, when the time came, to stretch themselves on the ground as they were—the archers naked, the Servant in his silvery tunic. I was wearing my sleeping bag.

I couldn't sleep at first, but listened to the noises of the night. There were bird calls—pleasant, fluting notes, and the occasional harsh screech that immediately made me think *owl*. I heard a distant barking noise, too, carried on and on by a series of throats, that might or might not have been the dreaded wolves.

The rain stopped sometime around midnight. I remember thinking that it was a good thing the local day was a whole forty minutes shorter than a standard day, and that the night would therefore be a little shorter. It was the first good thought I'd had regarding local time, which had hitherto seemed to be against us. Twenty times forty minutes is more than thirteen hours... thirteen hours less time to make headway before our deadline expired and we were into phase two of the operation.

As I lay in the dark, some distance away from the red glow of the fire, I couldn't help thinking that here was a golden opportunity for the Servant and his henchmen to make a play. I was alone, not expected back for some time. It would be an easy job to overpower me, open up the suit, introduce infective material.

But then what? A take-over takes time. They could never use me as a vector to get the stuff into the ship...not without turning me into an automaton utterly subject to the will of a black dendrite—or their wonderful Self. And to do that, they'd presumably have to tip their hand by letting the stuff grow all over me....

They were stupid thoughts—the kind of half-rational ideas that always surface as you sink below consciousness toward sleep. They lacked sense and they lacked force, but there was no way I could keep them at bay.

Ultimately, though, they lost their feeble grip on me and I was asleep.

I woke into the first bright light of day.

The fire was nothing now but a pile of ash smoldering idly away. One of the archers was squatting before it, peering through the smoke into the distance. The others were asleep— or still, at any rate.

The sky was clear now, with only a few white clouds drifting on a mild breeze.

The archer looked up as I approached, without any obvious interest.

"Anything happen during the night?" I asked.

"A wolf came," he said laconically. "A scout for the pack. It went away."

"You didn't shoot at it?"

"I didn't see it. I smelled it."

"Will it be back?"

"I don't know."

I looked out at the expanse of the plain. There was a great deal of tall grass hereabouts, with a multitude of ragged bushes and twisted trees breaking through in clumps. It looked desolate and empty, except for small birds in the branches and high in the sky.

The dew was already rising.

I took out another tube of tasteless but nutritious mush, and began squirting it through the filter. In the meantime I walked the length of the ship, covering much the same ground as I had the previous night, but seeming to see it better now. I blinked the sleep from my eyes and tried to gather my senses, with my hopes somewhat renewed. When I got back to the fire the others were all awake, and the Servant was coaxing the fire back to life in order to make more tea. I passed by, determined to further the investigation. I paused here and there to sort through the debris littering the ground—the useless remnants of cannibalized machines. There was no shortage of rubbish, but most of it would only interest archaeologists excavating the site in a thousand years time. They could have a fine old time identifying every last nest of printed circuits with the aid of a microscope. I wanted artifacts slightly more recent then these. Arrowheads that were not city arrowheads...tools made out of large bones, that could only have come from beasts like the oxen....

But I was wasting my time. I had made the trip for nothing.

"All right," I said to the Servant, finally. "Let's go home."

We mounted up and set off on the long ride home. My legs were stiff and we hadn't gone far before I began to ache. The Servant, as he had the day before, urged his mount forward to take the lead, and when I tried to come up level with him he edged away. Mentally cursing him I coaxed my own animal sideways, trying to get closer.

The animal responded, as always, to the pressure of my hands and heels, but all of a sudden was halted in mid-stride.

I was catapulted forward. With neither saddle nor stirrups my position was precarious enough without sudden stops. I went head-first in an inglorious swan dive over the beast's head. The tip of one of the coiled horns caught my right leg just above the knee and I felt both the plastic of my suit and the cloth of my one-piece being ripped. I twisted slightly in flight and came down on my left shoulder, rolling over to avoid breaking either my neck or my back. The fall shook me up badly.

The ox also came down with a hell of a thump, but it had veered the other way in tripping and it didn't roll on top of me— if it had, or if one of its hooves had caught me, I might have been seriously hurt. As it was, I got away with bruises and a long scratch on my leg which bled a little but wasn't deep enough to cause any significant anguish. I was okay...but the beast wasn't.

I sat up, feeling very dazed, and saw the animal trying to rise. Its right foreleg was broken—the bone must have snapped clean through. The leg was flapping in a rather sickening manner. The poor creature had put its foot into the mouth of one of the multitudinous burrows that riddled the heath while I had been trying to urge it closer to the Servant's mount.

I shook my head, trying to clear it. Then I looked up.

The Servant had already dismounted, and he was quick to reach the stricken beast. The ox relaxed, and stopped trying to get up. It lay back as the Servant examined the broken leg. The archers, still mounted, formed a ring around us.

The dark man turned to stare hard at me, and for once there was an expression on his face...an expression of muted fury. I was still dazed and bewildered. But I came very rapidly to my senses when I saw that one of the archers was notching an arrow to his bow...and aiming straight between my eyes.

"Now wait a minute," I said thickly. "It wasn't my fault! It was an accident!"

The archer had paused. But it wasn't because of anything I'd said. He was hesitating...waiting for a decision. I didn't see how he was going to get one. The Self was a full day's ride away.

At last, I thought, *I get to witness some spontaneity. Decision-making ad lib.*

I only wished that I weren't the victim of the decision.

The Servant looked at me long and hard—at my face, at the torn plastic sheathing my leg, at the blood that was staining my one-piece. Then he looked at the beast. It took him a long, long time to make up his mind. Then be just glanced at the archer and shook his head.

I realized that I was holding my breath, and exhaled gratefully.

"It was an accident," I said again. "It could have happened to any of us."

The Servant transfixed me with a gaze that was almost venomous. At least I'd gotten a reaction out of him, though it was a reaction I couldn't immediately understand. The ox would have to be destroyed, of course—the broken leg would finish it. But why should a mishap to a beast cause such an upswell of rage in such an imperturbable individual?

"I'm sorry," I said. I felt obliged to say something.

The Servant was caressing the neck of the injured animal, which was quite quiescent now. Its reaction to the shock and the pain had been damped down...probably by the parasite.

I remembered what the Servant had implied regarding the beasts being part of the Nation along with the people. Was that the cause of the rage...as if I had caused the death of his brother?

Suddenly, it occurred to me to wonder what would happen next. I watched the Servant's hand as it slowed in its gentle movement over the hide where the black network was. The archers dismounted, and settled their mounts as if we were scheduled for a long wait. The Servant knelt down, adjusting his position so that he could be comfortable, and placed his other hand on the neck of the fallen beast.

Then I saw the black lines on his arm begin to move.

It was as though they were growing longer, or being stretched. The tips of the filaments that descended as far as the fingers themselves were lifted from the skin and began writhing like worms, very slowly...until they found their way into the matted hair of the beast's mane, into which they went as if they were searching for something.

And then I realized what a fool I'd been—what fools we'd all been—for not guessing what should have been obvious, for not realizing exactly what the situation in the City of the Sun was. I realized what the Self had decided to try and conceal from us, until one of us might be prepared to experience it for himself. And I realized why I had almost been shot...not because of the death of the beast but because I was about to witness something that would help me to understand the people of the city far more than I already did...and which would increase my fears proportionately.

CHAPTER TEN

We'd been misled by a simple illusion. We saw each man carrying a black dendrite and we'd automatically assumed that each man had a parasite. We'd automatically thought of each dendrite as an entity in its own right, an individual...despite the fact that we knew all along that it wasn't an *organism* as such but a community of cells. Split in two, it wouldn't have been in any way injured...it wouldn't even have become "two" communities, just one community divided. And you could continue that process of division as far as you liked. You could divide the community into a thousand bits, and it would still be one...it would still retain the ability to *connect itself up again.*

While I watched the Servant's black companion fuse with the part of itself that had been parasitic upon the ox, to draw off the ox's companion and leave nothing there but a wounded animal, no longer part of the Self, I realized that the City of the Sun was afflicted by only one parasitic community. The entire biomass of all the black dendrites functioned as a single gigantic entity—not so much a pseudo-organism as a super-organism.

It didn't take much thought, now that the basic conceptual breakthrough was achieved, to work out how the Self made its decisions. All the people had to do was to hold hands in little groups. The parasite cells would fuse—and their brains would be literally and physically linked up by a multitude of skeins of mimic-nerve tissue. Like telephone exchanges. The brains, united, would form a group mind which would take into itself all the information and all the skills of the various individual minds, and distribute the synthesis around the group, so that each individual mind would become an echo of the whole. When a decision was to be taken the people got together in small groups, each group assessing the situation. Then each member of the group would go and join another group, and the synthesis would continue as groups of groups incorporated the question and distributed assessments and attitudes. It wasn't necessary for all the people of the city to come together simultaneously, any more than it's necessary for every single cell in a brain to be active at once. As long as people kept touching and separating, touching and separating, there would be free flow of information and attitudes throughout the population. Effectively, every single mind would have the pooled knowledge and insight of the entire community to draw on.

No wonder every single man and woman could understand every single one of the pictographs mounted upon the city walls. No wonder they needed only one physical representation of all that they knew and understood...and that only as a means of reinforcement, of constant support and unification of the community. Of course they needed no reference books, no data bank. No wonder their evasion of questions was so absolutely consistent and uniform throughout the city.

I had marveled about all the features of the life of the people that were significant of a hive mind. But after rejecting telepathy as a hypothesis I had discarded the notion as anything more than a metaphor. Not for a moment had it occurred to me that there could be a *physical* link between minds, and that the parasite tissue, with its faculties of mimicry and adaptive versatility, could provide such a link.

Now I saw, and understood.

They had tried to hide from us how different from us they really were. They had let us think that they were all individuals—unnaturally similar to one another, living in unnaturally perfect order, but still individuals. They did not want us to realize how real their representation of themselves as facets of a single Self actually was. They had hoped to appear harmless...strange, but harmless. They had hoped to persuade us that we stood to lose very little by the experiment of exposing ourselves to infection—allowing the parasite access to our bodies. They hoped to take advantage of our confidence in our medical resources, our genetic engineering facilities.

But once one of us was infected...sufficiently infected to enable the brain-to-brain linkages to be set up...then we would have been led to the full and complete understanding that was promised. We would have become part of the Self.

Totally and irrevocably.

Our minds would be sucked into the group, the group's mind would have flooded our brains. It would probably take no more than a few moments, once the parasite was established.

And then our volunteers, whoever they were, would return to the ship full of assurances about there being no danger, nothing at all to worry about. Not slaves or automata, as we had feared in our primitive way, but merely parts of the Self, engaged in the routine business of Self-interest.

I dropped my eyes from their fascinated study of the Servant recovering the companion from the doomed ox, and stared instead at the foot-long rent in my protective suit. I felt suddenly very sick...and the feeling had nothing to do with the sight of my blood oozing sluggishly from the scratch that ran across the side of the knee.

I noticed then that the archers were peering intently westward, staring into the bleak wilderness. The wind was blowing that way...carrying the scent of blood. The beast's blood, and mine. I recalled the archer's laconic revelation that there had been a wolf prowling around the camp during the previous night.

I got slowly to my feet, and walked past the injured ox. The Servant was in a virtual trance, and was as still as a statue.

"Are the wolves still nearby?" I asked the bowman who'd stood guard before the dawn.

"They will not have gone far," he replied.

"Will they attack?"

"Possibly."

I followed the direction of their gaze with my own eyes, but there seemed to be no movement.

"Shouldn't we build a fire?" I asked.

"There is not time," came the reply. "And fire is not so frightening by day."

He didn't sound in the least fearful. I sat down again, and inspected my leg carefully. It would be no problem, but I had to sit still for a while to allow the blood to clot. Time dragged by, and the stillness seemed pregnant with menace. The tableau of man and beast seemed frozen now—there was no movement of the black threads now they were joined. Cells were moving, probably inside the outer tegument, but there was no gross movement of the whole structure. There was no way to guess how long the recovery would take because there was no way to guess how extensively the parasite had developed inside the large host body.

I began to feel thirsty.

Then I heard the baying of the pack and knew that they were on their way.

I was overcome by a sensation of helplessness. I had no weapon—not the slightest means of self-defense. There was no contribution I could make to the coming battle, if battle there was to be. I wanted to get on my mount and ride away, but the mount that had been mine was on its way to a merciful death.

The carnivores approached quickly, but stealthily. They were close before I saw one scuttling from the shelter of one tattered bush to another. It looked more like a hyena than a wolf, with skin dappled ochreous yellow and muddy grey, and a rounded head with squat muzzle and round ears. There was no way I could count them—there might have been four or forty.

They didn't charge in all at once. They spread out to surround us, and circled, taking a good long look at us from a range of fifty or sixty yards, ducking from cover to cover, poking their heads up every few moments.

The archers had arrows notched to their bowstrings, but they waited patiently, quite relaxed. The range was too long and they had no chance yet to get a reasonable sight of the enemy. As the beasts circled us, so the bowmen spread out, forming four points of a square, with myself, the Servant and the injured ox in the middle. The other oxen also spread out, and began to move back and forth along the lines of the hypothetical square. I was fascinated by the purposeful nature of their movements. They were neither frightened nor restless. They were under control.

What effect does contact with a supermind have on an animal? I wondered. It can't become intelligent—the brain hasn't the carrying capacity. But contact with the Self might allow it to make the most efficient possible use of what it has... most efficient, perhaps, in terms of the Self's priorities.

Their horns weren't built for stabbing, but rather for butting and tossing. I could have wished that they were better equipped, but I had the feeling that in a hard fight they'd be no mean allies.

The predators showed themselves more frequently as they crept ever closer, and I was able to get an increasingly better estimate of their strength. I formed the impression that there were between fifteen and twenty-five.

If I was right, they had sufficient numbers to do us a lot of damage—if they followed their present cautious tactics until they were close enough for a quick dash, and then all charged simultaneously.

But that wasn't their way.

One dog, bolder than the rest, finally broke cover for too long and tried to run diagonally for a clump of stiff-stemmed plants only twenty feet away. One of the archers let fly and the arrow caught the beast just behind the shoulder. It rolled over and made a terrible mewling sound. It lay on its back, kicking. The bolt hadn't killed it outright, but it had sealed its fate.

Meanwhile, the others ducked and dodged. But the example of what had happened to their unfortunate comrade didn't deter them. If anything, it seemed to excite them. There was more blood smell in the air now, and the blood of their own kind was apparently just as much a stimulus as the blood of a natural victim.

Another archer released an arrow, striking a wolf in the leg—again the wound wasn't fatal, but again it stopped the predator, which turned to limp away, the arrow catching in the grass as it ran.

Then the rest came, in groups of two or three, the runs not timed at all. Three were taken out by arrows, then a fourth... then the rest were at the perimeter of the defensive square...and the yak-deer went into action, heads down and hooves plunging.

Suddenly, everything was chaos, with the archers unable to get in a clear shot. They retreated inward, arrows notched so that they could let fly at point-blank range if a wolf came close enough for a final leap. And the wolves were leaping, jaws agape, at their natural prey, the oxen. Their strategy—attacking in small groups—was geared to pulling down herbivores cut out from a herd. They could stand being tossed and bruised, and while one occupied the horned head the others would dive for the legs or jump at the neck. But the head wasn't the only weapon the oxen had, and their forelegs lashed out to bowl the marauders over.

Another arrow thumped into flesh, and another. The archers didn't miss now. Despite the confusion they were picking their targets—wolves that had been knocked aside and were rolling on the ground, showing their pale underbellies and momentarily vulnerable.

Then, out of the corner of my eye, I saw one of the dogs make an absolutely prodigious leap at the shoulder of one of the mounts, its jaws clutching at the shaggy mane. As the long canines closed on a mouthful of fur the ox wheeled and bucked. One horn caught the wolf in the flank and turned the mighty leap into a soaring acrobatic arc. Thrown sideways, the wolf came plunging down into the center of our defensive circle...to land squarely on top of me.

I got my arms up to shield my face, but I was knocked flat by the weight of the descending body. The wolf was as surprised as I was, and he was falling sideways, so the jaws—still trailing long brown hairs—snapped shut on the empty air. I tried desperately to thrust the thing away, just to get rid of its presence, but all I did in rolling its body off mine was to turn it over and give its feet a chance to meet the earth and right its body. I was flat on my back by this time and in the worst position possible for self-defense. All I could do was grab a handful of the skin about its throat and push up, trying to force those dreadful teeth away from me. There wasn't much skin to spare but I managed to shove the head up anyhow. The creature jerked free and stabbed with its head, but it had lost coordination, and it didn't manage to get in a bite. Saliva flecked the plastic of my no-longer-protective suit, and the great yellow rows of teeth opened up again like a gin-trap.

There was nothing more that I could do.

And then an arrow, driven with tremendous force, went deep into its right eye and penetrated its brain. Its head went up as if someone had cracked its spine like a whip, and one single convulsion was all the life left in it. Then it was stone dead, and it fell across my chest like a great wet sandbag. It knocked the breath out of me, and I had to fight for air, cursing the awkward filters which seemed to be strangling me as tears squeezed into my eyes and there was a moment of pain in my lungs. Then the breath came back, and I sucked the air gratefully. I felt as if I'd just been beaten up, but I also felt an intoxicating lightness of mind—the relief of being alive.

I managed to heave the corpse of the wolf aside, and sat up.

The battle was over. The enemy was in full retreat. I counted six corpses, including the one beside me, and the first casualty of all was still where it had fallen, still thrashing around in the hopeless attempt to dislodge the arrow from its shoulder.

I didn't know which of the archers had fired the arrow which saved my life. I said "Thanks" loudly, for all of them. I couldn't help tempering my gratitude by wondering whether it had been a shot fired purely by reflex. Maybe if they had had a chance to think about it they would have considered it safer to let the beast kill me. It was a sour thought, but I was still feeling very sour.

The Servant didn't seem to have moved a muscle. He might have been totally oblivious of the whole thing. The oxen, too, were very calm now. They had done their job, neatly and effectively.

I felt bruised, but not any more bruised than I had been before the wolf fell on me. No doubt I was bruised after the crashing fall I'd had. But otherwise I was fine. It was going to be an uncomfortable ride home—always assuming that I didn't have to walk—but I could stand that.

The Servant came out of his trance, and I saw that the black network was no longer visible on the ox's neck beneath the shaggy fur. All gone, into the big black spider web under the silvery tunic. The Servant didn't look any bigger, but as he came to his feet he looked distinctly tired. He was probably near to exhaustion. All the energy to absorb the companion from the injured beast had been provided by *his* system. The parasite had no reserves of its own.

I looked down at the ox.

It was perfectly still. Dead.

Euthanasia without a bullet—the last merciful gift of the departing companion.

I looked into the drawn face of the Servant, and said, yet again: "I'm sorry."

There didn't seem to be anything else to say.

CHAPTER ELEVEN

They gave me one of the other mounts, while two of the bowmen doubled up. This time, I didn't make any attempt to bring myself up abreast of the Servant. I didn't have to. This time, he wanted to talk to me, and it was he who dropped back.

"It was not intended that you should see what you saw today," he said. Now it was his turn to make provocative statements. He wanted to know just how much I had inferred from the knowledge that the parasite communities could link up.

"And I was almost killed because of it," I retorted.

"The arrow was not released," he pointed out. "And another arrow saved your, life a few moments later."

"Do you intend to let me return to the ship?" I asked bluntly.

"You are free," the Servant informed me. "I have to act as I believe that the Self would decide. If I am wrong...then I will be punished. But I cannot force you to come to the city while a decision is made."

"What constitutes punishment?" I asked.

"That is not important," he replied. I disagreed. If making the wrong decisions was punishable, that implied a degree of independence of the individual from the Self. The nature of the punishment might tell me something about the incidence of the misdemeanor. But if he didn't intend talking about it there was no future in pressing the point.

"Why did you try to keep secret the fact that the dendrites were all part of the same super-individual?" I asked instead.

He knew what I meant, despite the improvised term. "Because

we knew that the idea would frighten you even more than what you had already seen," he said. "We knew that to you we seemed alien, that our companions seemed to you to be ugly parasites feeding on our substance, interfering with our bodies and our minds. We knew that even if your ship did not have the power to destroy the Self, Earth did. It was—and is—desperately necessary that we should persuade you that what has happened to us on this world is not evil—that, in fact, it brings us closer to God. While you saw the companions as individuals there seemed a good chance that you might see them as symbiotes, and that you might find the courage to risk one or two of your number to test the notion. We feared that if you knew the whole truth...that there is only one companion, which is companion to us all...you would see the situation differently, and consider the companion much more dangerous. At the individual level, you saw the dendrites as something that could be handled. But now that you see one vast creature, awesome in its proportions, you may no longer see it as something that you can cope with, if necessary. Your fear has increased...and the chances of your submitting to the terms laid down in our agreement are much less. That is true, is it not?"

"Yes," I admitted. "It's true. I might have been prepared to let a parasite grow on me...but I won't surrender myself to the power of tens of thousands of other minds, physically linked to mine. I'd stand to lose everything that I am. There's no way I'm going to put my identity into a circuit like that."

"You are wrong," he said. "You cannot understand. Without experience, there is no way you can know...not simply the truth about *us*...but also the greater truth."

"Have you ever considered that your God might be something black, with a million tentacles reaching into your minds, manipulating you to its own advantage...deluding you?" It was a bitchy question, but I figured that the time was right for asking it.

"You do not understand," he repeated.

He was right. Not merely in the sense that his statement was true, but in the sense that he had the commitment of total faith. He was absolutely sure of his own rightness, and any attack upon it, any questioning of it, just bounced off. It was impervious to doubt. His world view was a closed, self-supporting system. Most religious systems are. They make themselves invulnerable to reason by discounting it even as a method of thought. *Faith* is what is necessary...reason is just a way of cheating yourself. Even when the data defy your very senses, there's always a way out.

God moves in mysterious ways.

All gods do. It's the only way they can work.

Their religiousness was probably inevitable. Belief in God is an elementary form of selflessness—the acknowledgment of responsibility toward a hypothetical Other. In this case the process had worked the other way.... When selflessness and responsibility to a real Other become facts of life, so does God. It is no longer necessary to invent him. He exists.

"You say that you came here to learn about us," said the dark man. "All that we ask is that you do that—in the only possible way. You *must* open yourself to knowledge of the Self, you must join *with* the Self. Then you will learn. Then you will understand. Your thoughts now are governed by your nightmares. If you cannot control those nightmares, then we are all heading for disaster. You cannot go on thinking with your narrow prejudices. You *must* learn to understand."

The whole routine just went in one ear and out the other. I'd heard it all before. It was a sales pitch that had been running throughout history. Believe as we do and you will be saved. Continue as you are and suffer eternal damnation. Join us...or there will be strife, and war, and catastrophe. It was a call that never altered, the plea of faith to the doubter.

The only trouble was that there almost always *was* strife, and war, and catastrophe. And right now I could see the situation here on Arcadia heading for a grade-A disaster. *Daedalus* versus the City of the Sun. The genetic engineers versus the almighty parasite.

The last time I'd heard a pitch like the one the Servant had just thrown at me it had been thrown on behalf of the neo-Christian revival, by a boy named Peter, who was my son. As soon as the pitch was made we were lost. Strife followed, as easily and as naturally as night follows day. Now, he and I were virtually strangers. It had happened almost overnight. The only way that even such a tiny disaster as that could have been averted would have been total capitulation on my part. I hadn't been able to do that. I hadn't been able to close my world and accept faith as a substitute for reason. Much less could I capitulate with what the Servant was asking me in his capacity of missionary for the Self. There was no way, no way at all, that I was going to put my mind at risk, let it dissolve into some corporate mass.

And that being so, what chance could there be to avoid disaster?

They obviously still had hope. The arrow had not been released. Another had saved my life. I was free to return to the ship, carrying both the bad news and the urgent plea. But it's always the faithful whose hope lasts longest. Because they know they're right, and in their heart of hearts they believe that everyone else must see that they're right too. Persistent denial comes to seem, in the end, like simple perversity, which they are duty bound to punish...with the clearest of clear consciences.

I looked desperately for a hope to match the Servant's.

But I, poor doubter, couldn't find it.

It just didn't seem to be there.

I got back to the *Daedalus* in the late evening, just as it was getting dark. I stripped off my torn suit in the lock and dutifully underwent the full—and rather uncomfortable—decontamination procedure. Then I put on a new suit. I was certain that it wasn't necessary, but for the sake of taking not even the slightest chance, and for the peace of mind of the others, it seemed the best thing to do.

There wasn't exactly a welcoming committee waiting for me. Only three people were in the main cabin—Nathan and Mariel, who were sitting with a pile of paperwork, and Pete Rolving, who was sipping coffee. They did, however, stop what they were doing when I limped in.

"Hello, Alex," said Nathan. "Have a good trip?"

"No," I said.

"Did you find anything out at the ship?"

"Not a thing." I sat down.

"What's the matter with your leg?" asked Mariel.

"I fell off my trusty steed...right over the horns. It's nothing. Just stinging a bit from decontamination."

Her eyes gazed into mine, looking straight through me. She pushed her papers aside.

"I'll get the others," she said.

The tone of her voice told Nathan that this was not the time for listening with half an ear. He put his pen down and began to shuffle up the papers into a tidy pile.

"Get me some coffee, will you, Pete?" I said. "In a tube. I don't feel like sucking too hard.... I'd rather squirt it through."

He got me a tube. Mariel brought Conrad and Linda out of the lab. They looked as if they'd been working hard for a long time. Karen appeared out of the control room.

I gave them the story quickly, without bothering with any frills. The central fact was what was important. They could draw out the implications as well as I could. They'd be the same implications that had occurred to me in the morning. I was no longer so sure they were the right implications, but they were clear enough.

"They were fools to think they could hide this from us," said Nathan, when I finished.

"Why?" I replied. "If it hadn't been for the accident...."

"We'd have guessed," he said flatly. "All the evidence is there, all pointing in this direction. If it hadn't been for a natural predisposition in our thinking we'd have seen it right away. That barrier couldn't have held up for twenty days."

"I don't see that it changes things much," said Mariel. "Surely the central problem remains. Does the parasite have independent sentience or not? Is it active in the group consciousness or passive? Are the people being controlled...governed...manipulated...or not?"

"That may still be the central question," said Conrad pensively. "But it may now be more difficult. I don't mean more difficult for us to answer, because we had little enough chance of finding the answer anyhow, but more difficult to ask. It may have lost a lot of its meaning. While we were thinking about individual human minds, like our own, it was easy enough to visualize a situation of freedom and a situation of subservience to an external force or controlling sentience. We were assessing the situation relative to ourselves—using our own existential situation as a kind of baseline.

"Now that baseline is no longer relevant. We're talking now about a single collective entity...a Self-with-a-capital-S, with all that that implies. If we say now: is the human element of the collective dominant or subservient? we're trying to decide between two states which are, so far as we're concerned, just about unimaginable. The question has been removed *entirely* into the realms of the speculative. How can we discuss it meaningfully?"

"Come on," said Karen. "That's all high-sounding crap. Never mind philosophical hair-splitting. The question was and is simple enough to ask, even if it isn't easy to answer. Are the people in control, or aren't they?"

"No, Karen," I said, quietly. "Conrad's right. It was simple enough to say 'are the people in control?' when we thought we knew what we meant by 'the people'...that is, an assembly of individuals, the plural of 'person.' But now we don't know that any longer. 'People' is no longer plural, it's singular. The Self isn't just a fancy metaphor...it's something real. We now *know* that the individuals in the city are subservient—that they're dominated by a consciousness not their own individual consciousness. But we don't know and can't know what sort of consciousness that is or how complete its control is. We don't know that there's any *difference* between the kind of hive-mind they have and the kind of alien slave master control we hypothesized. Is one really the same as the other? Is the one just as bad, as evil, or just as good and beneficent as the other? What Conrad is trying to point out is that our *judgment* of the situation is no longer meaningful, because we have no basis on which to judge. Of individual slavery or freedom we can meaningfully say that 'this is bad' or 'this is good,' because we have our own situation and experience as a standard for comparison. Here, we no longer have that."

"What you're saying, in effect," said Karen, "is that it no longer matters whether the parasite's in control or not. Even if it isn't, these people are still enslaved...puppets dancing on their little black strings."

"That's an emotionally loaded, metaphor," I said. "But yes, what we're saying is something along those lines."

"Then our situation is surely clarified," she said. "We no longer have to worry about whether the parasite is sentient. It doesn't matter. We go all out to destroy it anyhow."

"No," I said. "Quite the reverse. We no longer have the ability to make judgments in this situation. We can't decide to destroy this thing...even if we could."

"Wait a minute," said Nathan. "Don't start digging trenches around the disputed territory just yet. Let's try to work it out a little further. As I see it, Alex, the people in the city were attempting to trick us. Their intention was to persuade us that it would be safe for one or more of us to allow ourselves to be parasitized, because the process would be reversible. Then they intended to induct the volunteer into the Self, at which point he or she would become available as an agent of the city. The ultimate aim would be to seize the ship and take us *all* into the Self."

"Yes," I said, half-reluctantly. "I guess that was their plan."

"And we have to remember that this thing didn't take root here in every member of the population simultaneously. It grew. Now in a colony full of individuals imbued with the pioneer spirit, can you imagine each and every person deciding that he'd like to become part of a collective mind and meekly submitting to parasitism? How do you suppose the Self co-opted the entire colony, Alex? They didn't have plastic suits or a solid steel hidey-hole.... It would have been easy. But the important question is whether the Self called for volunteers or whether it went all out to co-opt everybody regardless of individual choice. What do you think?"

"I guess there was a *coup d'état*," I said. "The Self followed its own priorities. It didn't encourage dissenters."

"That's the way I see it, too," he said. "Now, the point of all this—as you must surely have realized—is that the Self obviously doesn't feel inhibited when it comes to the matter of making judgments. It doesn't worry about whether it's morally or logically entitled to make decisions relative to individual states of consciousness—it just gobbles them up. You say that we can't take a decision in this matter, because we're not in a position to understand what has happened here. But I suggest to you that we *must* be prepared to make a judgment, because to make no judgment at all is simply to condone the kind of judgment the Self makes.

"Maybe that doesn't matter here and now. *We* can go home right now and leave this thing to its own devices. But there won't always be one city...and maybe not even one world. In a couple of hundred more years the Self could build starships of its own. It could send out its own colonies. It could send a *Daedalus* mission back to Earth, to offer us help. You know what that help would be, Alex. Induction into the Self.

"There's no neutral ground any more, Alex. You must see that. In view of what you've told us we have to act. We have a simple choice...either we try to destroy this thing here and now or we report back and pass the buck to Pietrasante. It will come to the same thing in the end. You know as well as I do that the UN doesn't take chances. They won't be content with destroying the parasite in the city. They'll destroy the world. They'll sterilize it completely. In fact, that's what they'll probably do anyhow, unless we can take back conclusive proof that the menace is averted."

For a few moments, I just couldn't speak. There was a foul taste in my mouth.

"I think you're wrong," said Conrad, in the meantime. "They wouldn't order the destruction of a world. Not on evidence like this. There'd be an outcry. There are people in the UN who wouldn't be prepared to admit that this was any kind of danger. There'd be people who'd find the idea of the Self very attractive. Earth is a sick world right now.... The search for alternatives has reached desperation pitch. They couldn't keep this a secret...it'd leak out. The UN's committees are too large and too heterogeneous to allow secrecy. Bombing this life system out of existence is something that could never be made acceptable to the world at large."

"That would depend," said Nathan, calmly, "on how the situation was put to the people. If the threat were imagined in the right terms.... It's all a matter of public relations."

"You're insane!" I said. "You *want* this to happen?"

"No," he replied. "No, I don't. I'm just pointing out that this is the alternative. Perhaps, as Conrad says, it's not absolutely certain. But it's a possible alternative, a plausible alternative, and to my mind a probable alternative."

"Alternative to what?" asked Karen.

"Alternative to our making our own judgment, of course. That's what I'm arguing for. I'm saying that we must judge, because if we don't someone else will. And we're in the position that counts. We're the ones who can make a judgment most accurately. We're here, dealing with the reality. The UN is at home, dealing with possibilities. What I'm proposing is that we should make a decision and then take it home in order to justify it. If we present the UN with a firm decision that we've made and carried through then we can make that decision stick. What I want to do is to destroy the parasite, if possible, without destroying the people or the world. Conrad has already pointed out how that might be done—find a gene group that will stop the parasite infecting new hosts. Protect the next generation from infection. Then the Self will slowly die with the present generation."

I knew even as he said it that it was a hopeless cause. It simply wouldn't work. Sure, we might design an artificial chromosome segment and a carrier virus to transmit it through the population of the city. Sure, it would render the newborn immune from infection. But for how long? The parasite community had countless billions of individual cells, each one an entity in its own right, with a generation time measurable in hours. What kind of mutation rate would be necessary for it to find a way round the immunity? Nathan had no conception of the rate at which the parasite could evolve if faced with a challenge. It wouldn't need sentience...just time.

But I wasn't going to tell him that. No way. I only hoped that Conrad and Linda would keep *their* mouths shut.

"You say that we have to make a judgment," I said. "You say that if we make up our minds, we can take back a fully prepared case and can argue until doomsday in support of our actions. All we have to do is stick to our guns, right?"

"If we make a decision here and stick to it," he agreed, "we have every chance of making it stick back home. That's much better from every point of view than if we pass the buck back. It's better in terms of the present situation...and it also gives us a slim chance of following through with the purpose of the mission. We have to show that we're capable of handling this problem and all the problems that men are likely to meet out here in the star worlds. While we maintain that image of complete competence we still have a chance of getting the colony project restarted...and that's what we were commissioned to do."

"Then let's not rule out the third alternative," I said, ignoring the second part of his statement, which was pitched artfully at my sympathies. "Suppose that we did pass judgment here, and decided that the city should be left alone, and that the people should be allowed to get on with their little existential experiment. Suppose we took that decision home with us and fought tooth and claw to defend it. Couldn't we make that stick? You say yourself that it's basically a matter of public relations...

just a matter of choosing the right words, applying the correct emotional resonances. You're supposed to be a real hotshot in the persuasion business...couldn't the great Nathan Parrick sell that to a bunch of clumsy, confused UN committees?"

He drummed the tabletop with his fingers for a few seconds. Nobody else jumped into the gap. We were between rounds in a title fight, and everyone recognized that it wasn't a free-for-all. Not just at this moment.

"Maybe I could," he said finally, "if I had some ammunition to use. But first you'll have to convince me. I think this thing is dangerous. Terribly dangerous. I want to see it stopped. I'd rather do it my way than the big bomb way. But at present I'd rather do it the big bomb way than take the kind of risk you want to take for the kind of reasons you have. Your conscience is a liability, Alex. You're the kind of man who'd think twice about killing a tiger while it was charging you. When you can't square a decision with your morality your immediate reaction is to let well alone...to withdraw. That's a kind of cowardice, Alex. You're saying that because we don't fully understand this thing we should let it be. It's not for us to decide. Then who is it for? Not the UN.... You don't want to pass it back to them, because they're likely to be tougher than I am. Who, then? God? But we know whose side God's on, Alex, and it isn't ours.

"This is no time for going weak at the knees and bleating that we have no right to pass judgment. We have every right—and we must. Because we're here. And as far as I can see that decision can only be one way. You know how it feels to be faced with destruction, Alex. Out there today you were under the jaws of a wolf. What did you feel just before that arrow killed the beast? And what did you feel just after? Remember that the wolf was only doing what nature intended, following its instincts blindly. Who are you to judge, who have no instincts to speak of, and are dominated by reason—black reason that grips your mind like a parasite? Who are you to judge, when you can't possibly understand? We have a wolf here, Alex, and I want to kill it. I intend to kill it."

"I think you're wrong," I said. "It's no wolf. Your analogy is vicious rubbish. What we have here is human. Maybe it's not like you or me, but it's human at least in part. It has its own morality. We don't have to destroy it...we can try to come to terms with it. Maybe that won't be easy. Maybe it will be very, very difficult. It might be impossible. *But we have to try.* My reluctance to judge isn't cowardice, Nathan. It's courage. It's the courage which allows us to face up to our own ignorance and lack of understanding, so that we don't have to think in black-and-white terms or in crude and stupid analogies. *That's* cowardice—the refusal to face the universe on its own terms, but to impose upon it the fictions of our own narrow minds. I won't let you destroy this thing, Nathan. And without my help, you *can't.*"

Nathan didn't say anything immediately. He didn't drum his fingers on the table, either. He was frozen into stillness. He was angry, but only the hardness of his muscles was showing that fact.

"We have a present for you, Alex," he said, very softly. "Linda?"

Linda got up and went into the lab. My eyes followed her. Nathan's gaze remained fixed on my face.

She came back with a sealed tube. Inside the tube was a black smear. There was no need to ask what it was.

"Where did you get it?" I whispered.

"From a rabbit," said Nathan. "While you were away...we thought it best to begin work on the main problem. Conrad and Linda have been doing thorough analyses for most of the two days you were gone. I think you'll find they've accomplished quite a lot."

"As soon as I was gone," I said, with something of a croak in my voice, "you agreed on this...all of you?"

"I was against it," said Mariel, gently. "But the vote...."

"You make your decisions first, and then you try to justify them...even before you knew the whole truth. You've *always* been determined to destroy this thing. Because it's strange."

"Because its inhuman, Alex," said Nathan firmly. "We want to save the people of the colony. We didn't have much time... only twenty days. We thought we ought to learn all we could."

"I trapped the rabbit," said Linda. "No one saw me. They don't know we have the specimen. It's the right species."

I looked at Conrad. "Even you?" I said.

He shrugged. "We need all the information we can get," he said. "Whatever we decide to do. I'm not necessarily advocating destruction...but I think we need to have the knowledge and the capability anyhow."

"But you did it behind my back...while I was out of the way."

"Nobody sent you away," said Nathan. "It was your idea. You can't expect everything here to stop while we wait for your return. We're pressed for time and we took the decision. We've begun work...and we need your help. I didn't want this to blow up into a full-scale confrontation, and I'm sorry it has. But you have work to do. We have the specimen...and it's up to you to find out everything you can about it. Including how to fight it. It is a *fait accompli,* Alex. You can't pretend now that we haven't got it."

"No," I said. "No, I can't."

I stood up.

"Where are you going?" asked Mariel.

"Out," I said. "I have to get out of this damned suit. I have to wear it inside, for *your* protection. But after spending most of today with a rip the size of a shark's mouth connecting me with the outside world I don't think I need it out there. I want some air."

And so saying, I went out. Even on a mere five minutes' reflection it came to seem like a pretty stupid and rather inglorious exit, but I felt the need. After all that had been piled up on me in a few nasty minutes I desperately wanted to relieve the pressure.

And so I left my suit in the lock, and went out to face the cool night air of Arcadia on its own terms.

CHAPTER TWELVE

I didn't go far...just far enough to feel that I was apart from the ship, on my own. It was a clear night and the sky was full of stars. The Milky Way slanted across the limitless black field away to the south-east. I sat down on a cushion of the soft, waxy grass, and felt the stems with my fingertips, gently.

It was very quiet.

In my head, I made up stories. Scenarios, as the devotees of the science of prognostics call them. Scenario one looked like this:

On the planet Arcadia, in a pleasant country of temperate climate, colonists from Earth discover a miraculous herb which makes them healthy in body and allows them to link their minds together in mystical communion, achieving a supernatural harmony in the unity of a hyper-mind. They achieve the perfect democracy, with the collective will of the people responsible for all decisions, which it takes wisely and morally. The people build a magnificent city where they live a Utopian existence. Because of the nature of their experience in direct mental communion with one another they perceive that the isolation and loneliness of the individual sentient mind estranged from its universe is unnatural, and that there is a unity in all things, an integrity that binds every particle of the universe into a great system and a great scheme. They become aware—directly aware—of the existence of a divine plan, and they imagine a divine will which is the collective mind of the entirety of creation. Thus, they know God. They live as God always intended that man should live—as all intelligent life should live—in harmony, unaggres-sively, taking up arms only against the carnivores that prey on the flesh of other animals. They are happy.

Then the men from Earth arrive. Torn by the petty jealousies and uncertainties that haunt individual, alienated consciousness, with their emotional reactions and prejudices out of control, they are offended by what they find on Arcadia. Their aim is to destroy the city and the Nation—either to smash the collective hyper-mind and return the people of Arcadia to their primitive state of individual hell, or to obliterate all life from the surface of the world. These men are the most vicious of carnivores, the most wanton of killers.

After destroying Arcadia they go on to interfere with the divine plan somewhere else.

Scenario two looked like this:

On the planet Arcadia, in a pleasant country of temperate climate, colonists from Earth are attacked by the most insidious of enemies—a parasite which digs its way into their very brains. The cellular units of the parasite may connect into a pseudo-organism of any magnitude—into an organization of cells many thousand times the size of the human brain. Furthermore, the cells have the property of mimicry. Once having contacted an organ of such complexity and capability as the human brain the parasite can easily duplicate it and learn to develop similar func-tions. It acquires the faculties of conscious thought, intelligence and self-awareness, and forms a mind of its own which floods the brains of its victims, reducing their own personalities to helpless subservience to a single Self, which is its own although made in the image of the human individual self. Essentially, the parasite becomes a great brain with several thousand bodies. These bodies are organized by their single mind into a hive-like society with various castes differing according to division of labor. The super-mind has such control over its bodies that it can keep them free from disease and can also control devel-opment of various organs—thus many of the castes are made up entirely of males whose sexuality is undeveloped. They are specialized for their work like worker ants. The parasite begins a long program of controlled self-development and evolution preparatory to extending its domination to all other worlds where human colonies exist—and perhaps ultimately to all habitable worlds in the universe.

Then the men from Earth arrive. Although relatively naive they pose a threat. Firstly, they arrive at a time when the super-mind is still relatively undeveloped, having so far acquired only a fraction of the powers potential to it. Secondly, they have an impregnable base from which to operate, and within it a genetic engineering laboratory potentially capable of producing a living weapon which can destroy the super-mind. The super-mind therefore tries to hide its real nature from the visitors, and attempts to seduce them into accepting parasitism by pretending to be harmless. Once it has taken over one of them, by one means or another, it stands a reasonable chance of getting into the ship, at which point it has won the battle. The men from Earth, although realizing the true state of affairs, hesitate over the proper course of action, giving the super-mind time to plan a winning strategy. The men from Earth are absorbed into the super-mind and carry it back to an unsuspecting Earth, which is conquered with a minimum of trouble.

After taking over Earth, the super-mind goes on to co-opt the whole universe to itself and, effectively, to become God.

Maybe, I thought, *it already happened once, an unimaginable age ago, and life in the universe as it is today is the wreckage of the last super-mind, which somehow destroyed itself.*

There were other scenarios that came to mind, but not ones that I had to make up. They were real.

In the sixteenth and seventeenth centuries on Good Old Earth the Christian Churches became convinced that there was a vast diabolical conspiracy to turn the human race away from God, and that the Devil appeared to his minions at great Sabbats, to which witches would fly from far and wide to celebrate their degeneracy. It was believed that the secret society of witches practiced cannibalism and worked all manner of evil deeds by means of the supernatural power vested in them.

Thousands of people were tortured and burned.

Because of a fantasy—an imaginary threat created out of fear and political expediency.

In the twentieth century on Good Old Earth the Nazis in Germany became convinced that there was a vast conspiracy of Jews secretly dominating the world's financial and political affairs, and that the Jews were an inferior race preventing the destined masters of the world from coming into their due inheritance.

Millions of people were tortured and killed.

Because of a fantasy—an imaginary threat created out of malice and political expediency.

I realized that something which Nathan had said was true. It was for us to judge. For each and everyone of us. We couldn't pass judgment on the City of the Sun, because we simply didn't have the information we needed to reach a reasonable decision. But we could pass judgment on our own actions and our own emotions. We could, and we had to....

We had to mediate between two collective wills—the assembly of human minds called the UN and the rather different aggregation of minds called the Self. We were stuck between them. We could step back and let them confront one another directly. Or we could stay where we were, and try to save them from one another.

We could try to save the Self from the Godless fear of the UN, and we could try to save the UN from the righteous purposes of the Nation's God.

Someone touched me on the shoulder.

It was Mariel, plastic-suited for safety's sake.

"They're watching you through the camera," she said. "They don't like your being out here without a suit. Anything might happen. I know why you're doing it, but it's not much of a gesture. Come back inside and talk it over. Nathan's not so absolutely determined as you think. It's the way he presents things—he always argues to one side or the other, never down the middle. But he's still open to persuasion. If you can show that there's nothing to be afraid of you might win him over. But the only way you're going to do that is to work on the specimen that Linda brought back...and work out a way to fight it. Until we have some kind of defense against this thing, you're not going to persuade anyone to let it alone."

"And once we have the defense?" I said, bitterly. "What's to stop us using it to attack?"

"You are," she said. "If you can reduce our fears. That's what you're fighting—not Nathan, or politics, but the nightmares that jump into our minds when we meet certain ideas and see certain signals. You know what I mean. You've been through it yourself."

I looked up at her, but I could only see a dim silhouette.

"You voted against trapping the parasitized animal," I said.

"I didn't think it was fair to you. Nathan deliberately held back from raising the issue until you were gone. He was afraid that you'd want to stick to the agreement."

"Thanks," I said.

"That doesn't mean that I'm with you all the way. I have nightmares too...maybe more than the rest of you. I can read your fears as well as my own. Unless you can kill that fear there's no way you're going to save this world."

She was dead right, all along the line. I knew it. The only way to persuade anyone that this world should be left alone was to convince them that it posed no threat...or a threat that was bearable. The nightmares had to be vanquished.

Even mine.

There was only one thing to do. I went back inside, suiting up in the lock, and went straight to the lab to find out what kind of progress Linda and Conrad had made in their investigation of the parasite cells.

They'd been working round the clock, working together twelve hours of the day and each taking a six-hour-sleep shift while the other worked alone during the other twelve. In thirty hours they'd accomplished a great deal.

The parasite cells they were working with were, of course, independent of the pseudo-organism investing the people of the city and their domestic animals, and we couldn't be absolutely certain that it was the same species, or that even if it were the cells would exhibit exactly the same properties. It was, however, the species that I had singled out from the survey report as being the likely suspect. The rabbit-like creature hadn't yielded much of the stuff—once the black spiderweb was cut from its epidermis it was difficult to tell which of the internal cells were parasite tissue and which were host tissue. Conrad had already prepared several hundred sections from various parts of the host body, but hadn't found any definite way to tell the mimic cells from the host cells. Some were obviously invaders, but others looked to be borderline cases, suggesting a full spectrum of mimic accuracy.

There is, however, one advantage to dealing with communal pseudo-organisms rather than metazoan organisms, and that is that you can slice them up as fine as you like. The little spider web had been split into more than a thousand units, and Conrad had begun a whole series of experiments to discover what kind of tissues the stuff would grow on and how fast. He was using both tissue cultures for *in vivo* experiments and artificial cultures for *in vitro* tests. Linda, in the meantime, was running the biochemical analyses.

One thing that they had already found out—although it really only confirmed the obvious—was that the parasite cells had a chromosome count far in excess of any ordinary protozoan—or even most primitive metazoans. At any one time much of the gene system would be inactive, but versatility was built in to such an extent that it was a very large and complex system. There were thirty-two chromosome pairs—enough to carry the program of a sophisticated vertebrate. This discovery was, in a way, cause for hope. Complex gene systems are always delicately balanced systems, vulnerable to interference. The one problem was that interfering strategically and specifically would require a vast amount of analytical work. Three people with one lab couldn't possibly do it. We could interfere fairly easily with human gene systems only because two centuries of solid work had already been done on the human genotype and systems modification to give us a flying start. It would take about two centuries to obtain anything like a creative mastery of the parasite's systems.

I spent a couple of hours helping Conrad check his experiments, tallying cell growth and cell destruction in the many different cultures. This was the only kind of work where two pairs of hands working together could halve the work—the apparatus Linda was using was geared to the attentions of a single operator.

It didn't take long to confirm our suspicion that the parasite was unusually adaptable. In most of the living-tissue cultures the cells not only began to divide with some alacrity, but very soon began to differentiate as the mimic reaction was induced. The parasite took to human-tissue cultures—mostly contributed by Conrad—with somewhat less enthusiasm, but nevertheless the cells grew. Not unnaturally, the cells were far less happy in the ordinary nutrient cultures. A good many of the standard cocktails which would quite adequately support virtually all Earthly ectoparasites encouraged no cell growth whatsoever. Only a few of the most heavily protein-enriched synthetic media allowed the parasite cells to multiply. We sorted out a batch of these and began subdividing them as experimental media for testing various poisons. We also separated out several batches of the human tissue-culture experiments so that we could test the threshold effects of various forms of discouragement. It's no good finding out how to poison a parasite if you also have to poison the host.

All this was routine, but unlikely to be important in the long run. It might turn up something useful, but the possibility seemed to me to be slim. There was likely to be only one safe and sure way to inhibit the parasite from infecting people, and that depended on the biochemical analysis. Once we had a thorough profile of the organism's metabolic processes we would be able to identify anything from a few dozen to a few thousand simple proteins and fatty substances that were sufficiently different from those involved in human metabolic processes to be safe targets for attack. Having identified these, the standard procedure was to tailor short gene systems, usually of less than ten genes, which would program a strong bodily reaction against those substances. These would be incorporated into a virus that could be made endemic in the population, and the virus would then defend its host against infection by any parasite cell whose internal chemical processes involved the target molecules.

It was a procedure that had worked on other colony worlds, applied either by ourselves or by Kilner's team. It wasn't quite foolproof; cellular processes are usually very well confined and the leakage of molecules across the cell wall—both in and out—is often so slow that there is usually a "honeymoon period" before the defending viruses and the invading cells actually go to war. This meant that on one or two occasions when I'd used the technique against protozoan invaders the rate of destruction of the invader cells wasn't adequate to keep pace with the rate of proliferation and reinfection. Against a communal parasite, however, where the invader cells had to stick together to be fully effective, it ought to work well enough.

There remained, however, one big doubt in my mind relative to this specific case, and that was the versatility of the parasite cells. There was no way we could estimate the extent to which that versatility applied to the actual metabolic processes of the parasite. Theory said that mimicry is always a superficial phenomenon, never extending to the level of molecular processes...but I was haunted by the fear that this might be the exception that proved the rule.

Only time would tell. Maybe more time than we had. Linda could obtain a list of target molecules in a matter of days, but you can't build a virus in days. We would need several weeks, even if we all worked eighteen hours a day every day, to come up with a series of attack viruses. And then we would still have to test them in the tissue cultures. That would only take days, but the results couldn't be taken as conclusive until we had tested over a much longer period of time—and ideally, until we had tested in the real circumstances, to see if a living person could be protected indefinitely from infection.

Even after that, there was the mutation rate of the parasite still looming large as a threat to long-term success. It wouldn't take long for a new strain of parasite to emerge which could confound our viruses. And then a new series of attack viruses would have to be devised. And then a new strain...and then a new series...and so *ad infinitum*. That's the way it is with various classes of virus on Earth, and why—even in the twenty-third century—we still have no cure for the common cold.

I could see all the difficulties looming large, but there was no point in lying down and letting them crush me. When asked to do the impossible the only sensible procedure is to start at the beginning and keep going, in the hope that somewhere en route the impossible will become possible. You can't afford to be disheartened by the thought of deadlines. If it was anyone's job to get the deadlines extended it was Nathan's—he was the diplomat.

I threw myself into the lab work and tried to set aside the horrors of the general situation. For the time being, there was nothing I could do about them.

And maybe nothing anyone could do.

CHAPTER THIRTEEN

Now there were three of us in the lab we altered the sleep shifts to eight hours and took them alternately, so that there were always two of us at work. I took the second eight-hour shift, which didn't start until early the next morning. When I woke up I paused for a tube of coffee and something to eat.

Nathan and Mariel were in the central cabin again, still working away at their mounds of paper, with occasional aid from the screen and the computer. They were working on the pictographs, collating the information they'd gleaned. It looked like a long job—and not one that might be immediately fruitful.

"I'm sorry about last night," said Nathan.

"Great," I muttered, ungraciously.

"It's just that...you seem to spend your life in a dream. As if none of this is real to you, just a lot of abstract notions of purely intellectual importance. Sometimes I feel as if I have to go to extremes to make you see that it's real and immanent."

"And that real problems have to be solved practically," I said. "And we all know what constitutes a practical solution. I know the way the world works, Nathan. And I know this is real."

"How's it going in the lab?"

"How does it ever go? Slowly. Shouldn't you be out and about, talking to the natives about their broken secrets and their attempted treachery?"

"Not just now," he replied. "We're staying put for a while. Waiting."

"For what?"

"I think it's their move. We know now what they tried to stop us from finding out. We have cause now not to trust them. They were afraid of what we'd think if we knew the truth, and of what we might do. Right...now it's up to them to stop us from doing it. By persuasion. They have to make some kind of offer. If we went outside...then maybe they'd think it wasn't necessary to make an offer. Maybe they'd think they could apply a slightly different kind of persuasion. While we're in here, they're worrying."

"Very devious," I commented. "And suppose they don't come to us cap in hand and say they're sorry?"

"Then we wait. And keep waiting. You have all you need in the lab. Ultimately you'll come up with something we can use. Oh, I know it'll take weeks and months and God only knows how long...and of course you can't and won't guarantee your results. But we've all the time in the world. We don't ever have to go out again until we have all the cards we need in our hand. And even if they do reopen negotiations...we're taking no chances, Alex. None at all."

"I might have to go out," I said, blandly.

"Why?"

"Any of a dozen reasons. To get another specimen. To pick up a few mice for experiments on whole organisms. To gather some vegetation as raw material in extracting local proteins. We can't just wave a magic wand in there, you know. We have to have material to work on. It isn't easy conducting the kind of operation we're trying to mount with hardly two grams of specimen...and the fact that it has to be kept isolated at all times from the air of the lab doesn't help. We're working all the time through plastic membranes."

"All right," he said, soothingly. "What you need, we'll get. When it's necessary. All I'm saying is that we have to be careful. We don't know what might happen if we step out through the lock now. The agreement died."

"If they'd wanted to play it rough," I said, "they had plenty of opportunity. They saved my life.... They let me come back here to tell you all what I'd seen. Does that sound like all-out war to you? They still think that they can talk—persuade us to recognize their point of view."

"In that case," said Nathan, "they'll be along to reopen negotiations, in their own good time."

I shook my head, and went back to work. It was the safest and sanest course.

There was nothing new to do, and nothing to be discovered at this stage. It was just a matter of going on and on... checking, tabulating, looking at results. As the parasite grew on the cultures which permitted it to grow we tested our range of means of killing it. It wasn't easy to kill.... We found nothing that would neatly excise it from human tissue without wreaking havoc among the human cells as well. That was only to be expected.

Linda began to produce a list of the simpler molecules characteristic of the parasite's metabolic pathways. The unfortunate thing was that even at this level there were discrepancies between specimens grown in different tissues. The cells were metabolically versatile. There were still a lot of molecules that were present in every instance, but as we went further up the scale of complexity that list would probably get whittled down dramatically. By the time we got to molecules of such size and delicacy they could easily be singled out for attack there might be very few indeed that were inevitably involved in the creature's metabolic processes no matter what circumstances it was growing in.

The hours slid by with remarkable rapidity. Linda went off-shift and Conrad came back on. I let him take over the experiments he'd initiated and I took over from Linda. We ate on the job.

We didn't talk. We didn't get in one another's way. We'd established something like a perfect working relationship—inside the lab, at least. Outside we speculated, argued, compared ideas. Inside, we worked. When we did talk, it was to pass on information with the maximum efficiency and the minimum fuss. We just didn't notice the hands of the clock rolling round. I got tired, but I didn't pay it much attention. Once you settle your body and mind into a rhythm, then all you need is something to keep both your mind and your hands occupied. You can go on almost forever, falling into a kind of mesmeric trance.

When Linda appeared in the doorway of the lab again I simply assumed that the time had flown and that it was my turn to sleep. I was almost through the door when I noticed that she wasn't dressed for work, and that she was calling out to Conrad, too.

"What's the matter?" I asked. I looked up at the clock and saw that it was just before midnight, ship's time. The shift had three more hours to run.

"Karen dragged me out of bed. There's someone outside the ship. And he isn't from the city."

It took a moment to sink in. I still had to change gear, mentally, and the automatic transmission just wasn't working.

"Not from the city," I repeated, trying to make the words divest themselves of their meaning.

Then I got the point.

Everyone else was in the main room except for Pete, who was in the control room. There was an image on the screen being relayed by the external camera with the help of light intensification. It showed a man who was exploring, the area around the airlock with his fingertips, as if looking for a door handle or a crevice into which he could insert his fingers. His eyes had the glassy quality of the unseeing.

I moved round to let Conrad and Linda get into position, and found myself jostling Karen's elbow.

"He tripped an alarm with his body heat," she murmured. "I got a red light, roused Pete. Then everyone else, as soon as we got an image and saw...."

She didn't have to go on. It was obvious enough what she'd seen.

The man had hair...a lot of hair. He was naked to the waist, and the only thing growing on his body, so far as we could see, was thick, curly hair. On his chest and on his back. He wasn't very big, but he was wiry. His muscles were thick, with no fat on them. The hair on his head grew long, and was tied behind with a ragged piece of cloth. His beard had been hacked short.

He turned away from the ship's smooth outer wall as he seemed to hear a sound somewhere nearby, and we saw the whole expanse of his back. There was not the slightest sign of a black spider web.

He found the rim of the airlock with his fingertips, and tried to get his fingernails into the crack—a stupid, futile gesture, but one which served to communicate to us something of his urgency.

"It looks," said Conrad, calmly, "as if the parasite didn't get them all after all."

"You said you saw no sign," whispered Nathan, to me.

"I didn't," I assured him. "But what does that prove? You can't draw conclusions from an absence of evidence."

He knew that as well as I did. I looked across at him, and saw his brow furrowed in concentration. He was worried. This was something he had not anticipated. The city people had told him that there were no men outside the city. I had found nothing to suggest that there might be. The suspicion that was niggling away at his mind was quite straightforward.

Was this a trick?

"That hair didn't grow overnight," I said. "And I don't believe that the city people can just take off their dendrites as if they were shedding a vest."

"Let him into the airlock," said Karen. "We don't need to let him any farther. We can talk over the intercom. But let him in.... He's scared. They may be watching the ship."

"And those archers are good," I said. "I wouldn't reckon on the dark to stop them."

"Did you ever hear of the Trojan Horse?" objected Nathan.

"He doesn't look Greek to me," said Karen.

"All right," said Nathan, swiftly. "Tell Pete to let him in."

With a little effort I could have resented his automatic assumption of command in this situation, but I let it go. He was making the only decision possible.

We watched the surprise on the hairy man's face as the outer lock slid back into its bed. He jumped back, and it seemed that he almost turned and ran. But he overcame his reflexes with no more than a moment's thought, and practically leapt through the opening into the chamber.

Karen called to Pete, and the outer door slid shut again. The image on the screen changed. It went dead for a second, then showed nothing but blackness. Then Pete switched on the light in the lock, and we saw the visitor cover his eyes with his hands against the brilliance. He slipped into a kind of defensive crouch. As soon as he could bear the glare of the light he peeped out through his fingers, furtively.

Nathan plugged a microphone into the panel beneath the screen and punched the combination to link it to the speaker in the wall of the decontamination chamber.

"Can you hear me?" he asked.

The answer was obviously affirmative. The man in the airlock jumped like a startled hare at the sound. He looked up, and his eyes fixed almost immediately on the speaker. The camera was just above it, and so he seemed to be staring straight at us from the screen. His hair was dark brown, almost black. His skin was tanned and leathery. The trousers which were his only garment apart from moccasins on his feet were made from the hide of one of the creatures we called oxen.

Before he answered he took another look around—at the shower heads, the controls on the decontamination unit, at the lockers where various pieces of equipment and the suits were stored. But he didn't touch anything.

"I hear you," he said.

"We can see you by means of a camera," said Nathan. "I'm afraid there's no provision for you to see us. But there's a microphone near the speaker. We can hear you clearly. I can't let you come any farther. Don't try to operate the controls on the inner door—they're frozen from the control room. You have to stay there. We don't dare let you in because of the danger of...infection."

"I'm not from the city," he said. "I'm from the north."

Nathan glanced at me. I shrugged.

"You came to find us?" asked Nathan.

"My name's Antolin Sorokin," said the other. "One of our men saw the city people at the ship two days ago. He saw the man in the plastic suit that was with them. We decided that it must mean visitors...from Earth. There was a big meteor some time ago."

"Yes," said Nathan. "That was us."

The hairy man didn't let him go on. "I had to come under cover of darkness," he said. "The archers might be nearby, though you aren't in their lands. And I had to come alone. If they knew I was here...."

Nathan put his hand carefully over the microphone, and turned to Mariel.

"Is he telling the truth?" he asked.

There was a moment's silence. Mariel was staring intently at the image on the screen.

"Yes," she said, finally, "I think he is."

"But...," prompted Nathan.

"I don't know," she said. "There's something a little bit odd. His expressions aren't quite...right. But it's not necessarily abnormal. I've met similar signs before, in people who just aren't socially...well-adjusted, if you know what I mean."

"But he's not lying?"

"I don't think so," she said. "And he certainly doesn't give the impression of being like the people of the city."

Nathan uncovered the microphone.

"Are you saying that the archers would kill you if they knew you were trying to make contact with us?"

"What do you think?" said Sorokin, harshly. "They shoot on sight. They'd hunt us down and kill every last one of us if they thought they could. But we know the territory better than they do. Did they even tell you that we exist?"

"No," said Nathan. "They denied it."

"They were afraid you might help us," said Sorokin.

I stretched my hand out, leaning across the table.

Nathan, after a brief hesitation, passed me the microphone.

"Are you immune to the parasite?" I asked.

He laughed, but without humor. "I don't know," he said. "I guess we must be. We avoid all possible contact with it, and we eat a lot of meat because we think that it doesn't like carnivores, but we don't know that either of those things is what stops us from being affected. Maybe we're naturally immune, maybe not. But we're free of the thing, and we do our best to stay free."

It was my turn to cover the mike. "If he is naturally immune," I told Nathan, "it changes things. It changes them a lot."

He nodded.

I gave the mike back to him.

"How many of you are there?" he asked.

"Six hundred or so," replied Sorokin. "We're not all together. Small groups, mostly. We move around a lot. If we settled we'd be vulnerable.... Those bowmen don't miss. There may be more of us somewhere else. Every now and again a few set out to go as far away as they can...thousands of miles, to find somewhere that they *can* settle in safety."

"But most of you stay here. Why?"

"There's a lot of game in the valley. It's easy living. We know the country, we know how to survive. Over the mountain...who knows what's there? But people try, as I say. Maybe I'll try someday. Maybe we all will. And in the meantime, if things are rough...sometimes we raid the city. Their fields. We always try to steal a little to store up for the winter."

"I see," said Nathan. "And now that you're here, what do you want from us?"

"Help," he replied.

"What kind of help?"

"We want you to help in the war against the city," said Sorokin, as if he were slightly angered by having to spell it out. "What else? You've seen them—you know what they are. Surely you'll help us, won't you?" There was a sharp note in his voice as it rose in pitch. For a brief second, it almost acquired the note that I associated with the unbroken voice of the dark Servant.

"If we can," said Nathan, reassuringly. "And you may be able to help us. We can find out whether you do have natural immunity...and if you do, then perhaps we can give you all the help you need."

Promises, promises, I thought.

"Come back with me now," urged Sorokin. "We can get away while it's still dark. I'll show you how things are up north."

Nathan didn't want to be rushed quite that fast. "What happened in the colony when the parasite first took hold?" he asked. "Can you tell us about it?"

"I wasn't even born," protested the man in the airlock. "I was born in a cave in the hills. Even my father and mother don't remember. What they say is that the black stuff just appeared and spread like wildfire. They couldn't find any way to kill it. After a while they got to ignoring it, because it didn't seem to do any harm. They found out that the black things could link up but it didn't seem to matter. It was only after eighty or ninety percent of the people were infected that it started getting into people's minds and linking brains. Then the people who had the disease had no choice but to live with it. They were trapped. My father's father and others of his generation stayed with the infected people for a long time, but one by one they were still coming down with it.... Nobody could be sure that he was immune. People started to leave. Others were thrown out by the infected ones, who'd taken up a lot of new habits, like vegetarianism, and discovered a whole range of new sins. In the end, they all left...all the ones that weren't infected. And now we live wild. The war's been going on for as long as I know and as long as my father knows. They're not human any more. To them, we're just carnivores—animals."

Even before he'd finished, Nathan had covered up the microphone again, and was checking with Mariel.

"It sounds reasonable," he said. "It could all be true. *But is it?*"

"You know there's no way I can be certain," she said. "I can't pluck his thoughts right out of his head. I can only pick up what I see. All I can say is that I've no reason to think he's lying. No guarantees."

"All right," he said. "We work on that assumption. Who goes with him?"

"How about you?" I asked, sarcastically.

He could have reeled off a dozen convincing reasons, but I already knew the real one. He didn't want to go because that would leave me in effective command here. He wanted to stay close to the city, and keep his iron grip on events aboard the *Daedalus*.

"Are you listening?" said Sorokin, who'd been left dangling in silence.

"We heard everything," answered Nathan smoothly. "We're just holding a brief discussion among ourselves—to decide who comes with you." He covered the mike again. "Someone's got to investigate this question of immunity," he said. "It had better be you, Alex. You said yourself that getting results out of the lab will take time. This new avenue may provide a shortcut. But you can't take Linda or Conrad with you—they'll have to keep up the work here."

"I'll go," volunteered Mariel.

"I don't think so," said Nathan. "There's still a lot of work here that you've already started. Karen can go."

"Sometimes," said Karen, "I resent this constant implication that I'm more expendable than anyone else. I get all the dirty jobs to do."

"Sure," I said. "But you'll do it. You wouldn't want me to go out alone to face all the dangers of the wilderness, now would you?"

"I suppose someone has to look after you," she muttered. "Get him out of the lock and let's decontaminate. Then I'll get suited up and we can join him outside. It's about time we had a little excitement."

Nathan spoke into the mike. "We're going to turn off the light and open the door," he said. "Wait outside. Two of us will join you in a few minutes. You have time to get well away before dawn."

The screen went dark, and then Pete switched back to the external camera. We saw Sorokin crouching outside, listening hard to the sounds of the night.

"Suddenly," I said, "I feel very tired."

"Take a pill," said Nathan.

"How?" I replied, bitterly.

He touched the tip of his tongue to the filters on his own suit. Then he looked at me and grinned.

"Good luck," he said.

"You don't believe in luck," I reminded him. "And neither do I."

"I mean it," he assured me.

I didn't know whether to call it diplomacy or showmanship.

"While I'm gone," I said, seriously, "you'll be sure and not pull any more shifty little tricks, won't you?"

"I won't," he assured me. He was handing out a lot of assurance. I was almost tempted to ask Mariel whether he was telling the truth.

But I was afraid of the answer.

CHAPTER FOURTEEN

As soon as the empty lock had gone through the normal de-contamination procedure Karen handed me one of two packs that she'd made up, and we went through.

We emerged into deep darkness. It wasn't just the effect of coming out of the light—there was a lot of heavy cloud obscuring the stars, and the only light was a very faint glow to the east—the sky's reflection of the feeble lights of the City of the Sun. We stood still for several moments, trying to acclimatize our eyes as far as was possible. We didn't dare use a light immediately lest we attract unwelcome attention.

In the end, we had to rely on touch in order to stay together. I put my hand on Sorokin's shoulder and held Karen by the hand. We moved slowly and carefully away from the ship, heading north and keeping the glow of the city lights to our right. We couldn't keep anything like a straight line because of the clumps of pulpy, yellow-flowered plants that strewed the hillside. In order to be as quiet as possible we had to take the route of least resistance, which wasn't easy to locate, although Sorokin did as well as anyone could have.

Soon we were going uphill, and I judged that we'd come too far over to the right—from the top of the hill we'd be able to see the city and the river. We were still heading in the right direction but I'd have preferred to keep on up our minor valley, with a nice big hill between the city's lands and ourselves. I whispered something to this effect, but Sorokin ignored it. I presumed that he knew what he was doing.

We'd gone just about three-quarters of a mile when they hit us. They came from all sides—we must have walked straight into their ambush.

I had one hand on Sorokin's shoulder and the other gripping Karen's hand. I wasn't exactly in a position to mount a valiant defense. A heavy body hit me somewhere around the middle and I was bowled over. I ended up on my back, pinned down. Karen, however, was in a better position. She'd had one hand free and she had obviously thought that it was free to be used. I'd have been carrying a flashlight in readiness for the moment that it was deemed safe to light up our way, but she had a mind that worked along different lines. She was holding a flashgun—a pistol with a parabolic reflector and a flare-bulb instead of a barrel. When fired it made one hell of a noise and a flash so bright as to temporarily blind an attacker, whether human or animal. It was a very useful defense, though it had one terrible defect—if your friends weren't expecting the flash it had just as much effect on them as it did on the enemy.

She fired it now without any warning. I tried to shut my eyes against the flare but my reflexes were too slow. The darkness was replaced by painful coruscations and an odd kind of sizzling sensation in my optic nerves. But I, at least, knew what had happened. It had happened to me before. The man pinning me down didn't and hadn't. He howled as if he'd been burned, and he jumped back. I staggered to my feet, made clumsy by the weight of the pack on my back. I didn't know which way to run—I couldn't even remember which way we'd come. I felt a hand grab at my shoulder, and lashed out with my fist. I felt it connect, and heard an anguished curse.

"It's me, you cretin!" hissed Karen.

The whisper was as much a mistake as the blow. I was promptly charged down again, and I heard the thud of flailing arms connecting with naked bodies as Karen tried to defend herself. Even blinded, the archers were determined to do their job. They'd recovered from the surprise.

In daylight, Karen's eyes might have been a big advantage,

but it's only in daylight that the one-eyed man can lord it over the kingdom of the blind. By night, having your optic nerves shocked into submission really doesn't achieve very much.

In short, despite the spirited defense, we still lost the fight. We ended up pinned down again, and then there was a long wait. I heard noises, but had no idea what was going on.

Then Karen said: "Can you see, Alex?"

"Are you kidding?" I replied, bitterly.

"*They* can. One of them just lit a candle. They recover bloody quickly."

I sighed. "It'll come back to me," I said. "In time. They probably have help in recuperating."

I felt myself lifted to my feet, and hustled off up the hill.

"Karen?" I asked.

"Right here beside you," she replied.

"What about Sorokin?"

"They got him too. He hasn't said a word. He didn't put up much resistance. But then, he's blind too...for the time being."

I didn't pursue the point. It wasn't the time to try deciding whether Sorokin was everything he claimed to be and had just been unlucky, or whether he was the Judas goat. Either way, we were on our way to the city. To the dungeons, if they had dungeons.

I felt a touch on my plastic-sheathed arm—the arm that wasn't on the side where Karen's voice had come from. The voice that followed up the touch was high and musical.

"I am sorry that it had to be this way," it said. "But there was no other."

I wasn't absolutely sure, but it seemed likely that the man who spoke was the Servant who'd guided me to the relic of the ship.

"Sure," I said. "God moves in mysterious ways, and if a little bit of stealth and violence seems called for...."

"You should not mock God."

"Is that a threat?"

"No," he said. "It is not a threat."

We staggered on.

"What now?" whispered Karen, in a conspiratorial tone. I guessed that the Servant had retired slightly.

"Oh," I said, airily. "You know the drill. With one bound Jack was free. Beat them all up a bit, run up the flag, and proclaim that henceforth Arcadia shall be a democratic republic. No trouble. Being blinded makes it a bit more difficult, of course, but no self-respecting hero lets a little thing like that bother him."

"It's a great plan," she agreed.

"True," I admitted.

Gradually, my sight came back. I even began to see the gleam of their lantern. By the time we reached the city's outermost wall I could see *them*. There were about ten archers—without their archery equipment—plus the dark-skinned servant. It seemed to me to be a sample of neurotic overkill. Half that number could probably have done the job.

We didn't climb all of the hill on which the city was built. Somewhere in the fourth circle we took a side-turning, and then went through a couple of doors into the hillside itself. It wasn't by any means a labyrinth—just a straight corridor to a big room set off from which were a number of cells. The heavy mob bundled each of us into a different cell. They bolted the doors on the outside.

The cells weren't as bad as some I'd seen. There was a toilet in the corner, and there was a table with candles and a tray. There was a chair, and a bed with a straw mattress. It was probably very cold, being so far underground, but I couldn't feel that, thanks to my insulation. The door had a square panel cut out of it a couple of feet square, with wooden bars. They didn't look like very effective bars to me. It wouldn't have taken the power of a superman to break them in two. In my experience the strength of a jail tends to vary directly in connection with the number of attempted breakouts. Obviously not many people tried to get out of this one. I peered through the bars into the big room outside. It had a big table and some wooden benches. There were none of the cushions that were strewn about so liberally in the pyramidal building where the Ego lived. I wasn't unduly surprised.

The archers and the Servant had all withdrawn. "Are you all right?" I called to Karen.

"As well as can be expected," she replied. I couldn't see her because her cell was flush with mine, but she was right next door.

"Sorokin!" I called.

There was no answer.

"Are you all right?" I added.

Still no reply. I knew he was there because I'd seen them bundle him in and shut the door. But he wasn't in a communicative mood.

"What happens now?" asked Karen.

"You're a great one for anticipating, aren't you?" I replied. "Always rushing to get to the next stage. Relax and enjoy the present...the future never comes, you know."

"Thanks," she answered.

"How the hell do I know what now?" I said. "I'm just thankful they haven't got a rack out there. If I really *had* to guess I'd say that we might be introduced to something small and black that will grow on us. But I don't have to guess, so I'll face that problem when I come to it."

It was a hypocritical little speech. I was facing the problem all right.... I was almost wishing that I could be blind to it.

After a while, the Servant returned. This time there were no archers with him—just three more Servants and the Ego. They all went straight to Sorokin's cell. I heard the bolts slide back, and all of the black-shrouded figures passed from my field of vision. Then I didn't hear anything else for a long, long time.

I gave up listening after ten minutes, and went to the bed. I lay down on the mattress. It wasn't overly comfortable but it was clean. And I was tired. Deliberately, I shut my eyes. The last thing I expected to be able to do was sleep—my intention was to shut out the world and all the nightmares that were looming up there. But sleep, strangely enough, came quickly to consume me. I guess when there are nightmares walking the shores of reality immersion in sleep can only be a release...or at least a strategic withdrawal, or whatever other euphemism you use to describe a full-scale retreat.

I was jerked awake by some small noise, which came accompanied by a strong sensation that something was about to happen.

I had no idea how much time had passed.

I was no longer alone—standing over me was the man who called himself the Ego. When my eyes opened he sat down on the chair at the table beside the head of the bed. I sat up. If we were going to converse we might at least be on the same level.

He rested one of his elbows on the table, and the black cloth of his tunic rustled.

"I am sorry for the way in which we brought you here," he said. "It was unfortunate, but necessary. We would not have resorted to deception had we not felt that the situation offered little alternative."

"Deception?" I queried.

"Come with me," he said, standing. "I will show you something. You should know the truth."

He went to the door, then paused, waiting for me to follow. I did so, a little sluggishly. He didn't take me far—just half a dozen paces to the next cell but one. As we passed Karen's door I glanced in. She was sitting on the bed, but when she saw me she bounced to her feet and came over. I raised my hand, half in salute, half to tell her to stay calm. I went to see what the Ego wanted to show me, in Sorokin's cell.

Sorokin wasn't there any more. In fact, he didn't exist any more.

They'd pulled the bed out from the wall, so that there was space on either side of it for two Servants to kneel. Together with the man on the bed they formed a kind of circle, all holding hands, all in some kind of trance. Their parasites were joined, too—and the circle was sealed because the black flesh had crawled across the back of what had once been Sorokin, and was ramifying gradually over the surface of his body. His hair had all fallen out. If it hadn't been for the Ego's mention of deception I might have seen it as a normal introduction procedure—the gathering of a new sheep into the flock. But I realized that what I was seeing was the reversal of a metamorphosis that had already taken place.

They had created Sorokin. The Self had invented him. The external ramifications of the parasite had been removed by absorption. Super-stimulation of hormonal and physiological processes had grown his hair. And his mind had been literally molded. He hadn't been pretending.... He had actually become a new person. He had been good enough to convince even Mariel.

"I never suspected that you could do something like that," I murmured.

"Nor did we," replied the Ego. "Until the necessity arose. We are only beginning to realize what we might do...and what we might be. Progress arises from the discovery of new problems. We have hardly begun."

"It was a very plausible story," I said. "Even though I'd failed to find the slightest evidence of others...I was ready to believe it."

"We were sure that you would," said the Ego. "When we realized what it was that you were searching for so earnestly at the ship."

"So you decoyed a couple of us out of the ship. It won't do you any good. You won't be able to decoy the rest out. No matter how convincing you are there'll always be two left behind. That's the one unbreakable rule."

"We do not need to bring any more of your people out. We only have to send one of you back in."

I watched the silent ceremony that was recreating one of the Nation's citizens out of what had been something very different—a programmed creature, an almost-perfect imitation of what he pretended to be.

"It won't work," I told him. "You have time on your hands and a good story that they still believe back at the *Daedalus*. But there's a radio in one of those packs you took from us, and we're expected to report in. When we don't they'll become suspicious. Given time, maybe you could program me as you programmed him—induct me into the Nation, destroy my individuality, set me up as you set him up, as a Judas goat. But you won't get me into the ship. Mariel knows me far too well—and she can read minds. You fooled her with an imaginary person, but you couldn't fool her with something pretending to be me...or Karen. You've wasted your time. You're no nearer to capturing the ship now than you ever were."

"That is not necessarily our goal," said the man in black. "Indeed, it would be a measure of desperation if we were to attempt any such thing."

"So what *do* you intend to do?"

"We do not yet know. It depends very much on what we learn concerning the nature of the situation. What we must do will depend very much on what your people intend to do."

That news didn't exactly fill me with hope. I knew what Nathan intended to do, and I couldn't suppose for one moment that the measures the Nation would take in return could be anything but desperate.

"You could have held me when we came back from the north," I said. "You didn't have to let me tell the others what I found out. Why snatch me now it's too late?"

"Perhaps it was a mistake to try to deceive you in the beginning," said the Ego. "But we undertook the deception with the most innocent of motives. We sought to protect you from your own fears and prejudices. Our aim then was to reassure you before welcoming you into the Nation in union with the Self. We have since seen fit to question the naivety of both the strategy and the ambition. Offering you time to study us also gave us the opportunity to study you. What we found changed our attitude somewhat. There was never any intention to use force, or to harm you. Such action was considered and rejected. The Servant had no option but to confirm and carry through that decision in the wilderness. He allowed you to return to the ship while he returned here to inform the Self of the new situation. In the meantime, we also discovered that you had obtained a specimen of what you call the parasite, in defiance of the agreement. You did not come out of the ship again, and we became concerned. It seemed possible that you might never come out— that you might stay within working on a means to destroy the so-called parasite. We feared that you might discover such a means. It therefore became necessary to lure out one or more of your number, so that we could find out what you intended to do, and how, and whether there is anything that we can do even at this stage to reach a reconciliation."

Considering it objectively, it sounded like a policy that made some kind of sense. But I was far from sure that it was the truth.

"It seems," said the Ego, turning away from the open cell-door, "that we have all behaved a little foolishly. We have been too narrow-minded in our approach. The Self was narrow-minded in its assumption that your absorption into the Nation was the only appropriate aim. You have been narrow-minded in your assumption that the Self is implicitly evil. The Self, we assure you, has become wiser through contact with you. You must remember that you are the first individual minds that the Self has encountered. When there were still individual minds on Arcadia the Self was at such a stage in its development that it was hardly aware of them. The story that Sorokin told you was, of course, untrue...but not so far from the truth. There were no immunes, but we believe the progress of the Self's growth in the colony was as described. The parasite, as you call it, came first, infecting everyone. Only when it was well-established did the possibility of linking brains materialize, and the first happening was certainly an accident. But once a link is forged...the cells that make up our companions are not intelligent, but they are highly active. They experiment, blindly, and let natural selection choose the effective results. When the colonists realized that the mind-to-mind link was possible, they may have done everything in their power to encourage it. They would have seen it then as something subject to individual control, a new faculty. The Self was generated by degrees. It has developed with astonishing rapidity, once given the chance to develop, but its origins are clouded even from itself. So are most of its potentials. I think that you may have assumed that the Self is something stable, something settled. That illusion was fostered, no doubt, by the fashion in which we have built our city. But in fact the Self is still in the process of evolving, and evolving very rapidly. This city was the product of its earliest burst of awareness and productivity. It is, we think now, a childish work. We believe that we will soon outgrow such infancy. It is our home, and we will live in it for many years yet, but the reasons which prompted us to build it are no longer so meaningful to us. When the Self began its first thought was to be itself. It did not imagine itself as something in the process of change. It imagined itself to be complete...and perfect. The flamboyant Utopian design of the city reflects this feeling. But the truth is that the Self knows not what it is or what it will become. It is changing and must continue to change, as every discovery it makes leads on to more and more. But you must not judge us even on the basis of what we seem to be, let alone on the basis of what you fear that we might be. Your minds are too narrow. You cannot know. Nor can we. Only God can know."

The rush of words stopped without having slowed down. I had been holding my breath, for no good reason. I let it go now, and inhaled deeply. I was completely at a loss. I didn't know where I was up to.

"What happens now?" I asked, consciously echoing Karen's question to me.

"We must find out what you know. We must discover what your friends aboard the ship are likely to do, and what effects their actions are likely to have."

"You want me to tell you everything."

"You *will* tell us everything."

I looked around the room. I still couldn't see a rack. Or a set of hot irons. Maybe they kept them in a cupboard somewhere.

"To judge by the way you said that," I said, dryly, "you have ways of making me talk."

He didn't appreciate the joke, but I heard Karen laugh. She was still at the door of her cell, hanging on to every word. It was a very bitter laugh.

"We must know the truth," said the Ego. "The whole truth."

"And nothing but the truth," I muttered. "I presume you have a truth serum."

"The Self," said the man in black, "is in a uniquely privileged position to study the effects of psychotropic drugs. I think you will understand why. You recall that our companion cells are fitted by evolution to be in a constant process of experimentation. The Self has inherited, on a mental level, something of that priority. The biochemical resources of Arcadia's life system are very rich."

"I'll bet they are," I muttered. The Self, he said, was only just beginning to realize some of its potentials. Every time it discovered a new problem it opened up a whole new spectrum of possibilities....

"I'm afraid that I must ask you to take off your suit," said the Ego. "We do not know what your intriguing filtration system would do to the drug. I give you my word that you will not be... infected...by the companion."

I wouldn't have given twopence for his word of honor. But I didn't even have two-pence worth of option. In a situation which offers no choice, you might as well give in gracefully.

"Here?" I asked.

"I think this is as good as anywhere," he replied. "And it may be necessary to return you to your cell...afterwards."

I went back into the cell, and slowly began to disrobe.

From somewhere, bang on cue, a Servant appeared with a bowl full of something that looked like runny porridge. Other Servants followed him in. There seemed to be quite a crowd. One of them brought in Karen from next door—she was allowed to keep her suit on. I presumed that in allowing her to be present they were doing me a small favor. I'd have a witness to consult later on about what had happened.

"The drug will send you to sleep," said the Ego, softly. "I fear the experience may not be altogether pleasant. Your *persona* may experience hallucinations of a vivid nature, subconsciously directed. The will, you see, must be detached from the memory, in order that information may be recalled accurately and mechanically."

"Forget the introductory lecture," I said. "Let's get on with it."

The Servant handed me the bowl.

It didn't *taste* anything like porridge.

CHAPTER FIFTEEN

I dreamed that I spent a night on the bare mountain.

It began with the wind, which howled mournfully in the dark pines, whose branches swung and swirled like dark whirlpools, while the tree spirits danced to the echoing music of the dashing air. The sky above was clear, but the mountain was an oasis in a massive ocean of cloud, protected by some supernatural force from a storm which raged all around with such fierceness that no traveler could possibly have come to the mountain from elsewhere without the aid of a supernatural agency. North, west, south and east the skies were tormented by lightning and the land was curtained by spiteful rain.

The witches flew through the storm protected by cocoons of impermeable shadow, assured of diabolical safe-conduct, borne aloft by demonic rams or goats, or black horses with flaring eyes, or shovels or batons thick-smeared with their anointments.

Fires sprang up around the mountain top, which burned violet and blue—fires which clustered round the pines but could not consume them, their flames and heat mere glamour confounding the darkness of God's night.

The Master did not fly to the gathering but simply *was*...born out of the black shadows of the mountain slopes, out of the very flesh of the rock. He was monstrous both in size and form, with great horns like a ram, the beard of a goat and the legs of a great ape. His feet were eagle's talons and his hindquarters were decorated like a male mandrill's. Light—white light—danced around his face like a shower of blurred sparks. His flesh was translucent. Beneath the flesh could clearly be seen the yellowed skull and the roundness of the bloody-humored eyes. And there were veins that stood out within the flesh like a vast web of thick, tarry strands, that seemed at once a cage for the inner being and a manifestation of inner decay.

The flesh of the face, all but invisible, held no expression which could be read or judged. But the eyes sat in the skull, and bulging bloody from their sockets seemed both terrible and melancholic...the fierce, despairing anger of perpetual misery.

As the witches arrived, one by one, they presented themselves to him, bowed down before him and kissed his parti-colored hindquarters. With their mouths thus embittered they turned to one another, and kissed one another. And their flesh became clear, its opaqueness stolen away by cruel magic, to reveal the whiteness of their bones and the blackness of their veins like grotesque creatures of the sea, writhing and coiling as they moved, splitting and recombining in the bloodlust of the evil kiss.

There were torments then, as witches who had performed insufficient evil were scourged with knotted ropes until the black veins burst the invisible surface of their lacerated flesh and oozed black blood. And every drop of black that fell remained alive, crawling like a worm into the crevices of the mountainside. All the while the witches cried the agony of their punishment, an echo of the divine retribution which would claim them all in time and send them to the ravages of misery that racked their host.

The feast, like its master, grew up out of the substance of the rocks. Coarse grass and stones and thorns and acid earth, pine needles and bird droppings, were englamored into meat and bread and sugar and spice. The mountain streams gushed with blood and wine recklessly mixed, and the devil spat fire into the mixture to make it fume. The witches ate, knowing that their fare remained yet what it was, despite appearances, and forced their savage joy to overcome the knowledge.

Then the celebrants dressed themselves in pantomime robes,

became caricatures of priests and acolytes and actors, caricaturing even the caricatures of their own lord which appeared in plays. They performed mockeries, not only of worship but of life and death and mystery, of custom and pleasure and artistry.

And the devil preached a sermon, with empty, unctuous promises heaped high, calling forth laughter and delight.

The sky made music for them, the thunder becoming a battery of drums, the wind playing countless flutes in the high branches, and they danced while the devil came among them, taking them one by one to the perverted consummation of their spiritual marriage. His prick, like the flesh of his face, was transparent, like a needle of ice, and he entered them with its terrible coldness, freezing the core of their very being and leaving them with the ecstatic pain of returning fire and feeling. And while they joined their blood flowed free, and mingled as the veins writhed out of the glassy flesh and closed in bizarre union.

On and on the Sabbat went, encapsulated in time within the sealed midnight moment, protected from the flux of the outer world by abstraction. And the timeless storm that shielded the secret place raged all around and terrorized the land.

After the dance they laid themselves down, with the devil oozing back into the rock to caress them all simultaneously with stony fingers and thorns. And the witches joined hands and touched their feet to one another's bodies, so that they became one vast interlocked spider web covering the animate mountain-cap, like a great living cloak.

They were entranced....

dreaming their own dream....

...while the devil bound his instruments together, with one self and one will, which was his own—utterly evil and utterly damned. He instructed them in wickedness, took their thoughts and instincts and made them subservient to his own fearful passion and mad intellect, scoured their souls in commemoration of the diabolical pact by which they had signed away their humanity in blood...a pact still written in every fiber of their substance.

I waited, hopelessly, for cockcrow.

Cockcrow never came.

For an infinite time, I was lost.

Later, I found myself night-flying, as they had flown, carried through the eternal storm but concealed from its violence.

All around me, the world went about its way.

Like a dead leaf in the vicious wind I was tossed and hurled, but I felt as light as the air itself. The hail and the rain hammered at my body, but the pain was held back, and I felt not the lightest touch. The lightning struck and struck at me, with all the jealousy of enraged divinity, like a maddened cobra.

Again and again and again....

But I was numb, through and through. The electric pain could not touch me, could not alarm my flesh in the slightest. Though it stabbed at heart and mind with frenzied desperation I was safe and secure.

I seemed to be falling rather than flying, but slowly...very slowly....

The pain that should have made me scream wound itself around me like a living creature, with all its torment reflected back upon itself. I was immune, anaesthetized. Had my skin torn and the blood flowed I could have watched, unworried. I could have watched myself torn apart and hardly cared. Something that was me was safe, and safe forever.

Looking down as I fell I saw two figures moving through the pines on the slope of another mountain, soaked by the rain and terrified by the thunder.

I knew their faces, but I couldn't remember their names.

As I fell nearer and nearer to the direction of their flight they became clearer and clearer, but I still could not put a name or an identity to them.

They were heading for the distant mountain, but they could neither reach nor escape the Sabbat. They would run forever, and get nowhere, with the terror too far ahead of them and hope too far behind.

Just before my fall carried me crashing into the multitudinous needles of the treetops, the vision dissolved. It collapsed, turned liquid, and drained away, its shape and structure altogether gone.

I realized that I was awake, though my eyes seemed to be glued shut. I didn't try too hard to open them. I was too exhausted. Instead, I tried to gather my reeling consciousness, to reassemble the shattered fragments of my being. I tried to listen. I tried to feel. I tried to remember.

I managed to get some sense of integrity again, to recover some sensation of wholeness. I could feel my heart beating in my chest, and the sound it made was I...I...I...I....

Its beat was measured, not panicked. It was under control.

I could feel cold air on the skin of my face, and a few droplets of sweat leaving cold scars as they evaporated.

It was a fantasy, I told myself. *Nothing but a fantasy.*

Then I let the monologue continue:

We lend too much credence to unreal experiences. We are too much affected by fantasies, even in the absence of belief. Belief is only necessary in the absence of understanding. But in the absence of understanding belief is necessary. The one thing we must realize is that we may choose our beliefs. We do not need to let them choose us, seducing us as fantasies.

If we cannot overcome our fantasies, what hope is there for us? In history, in eternity. Now and forever.

I opened my eyes.

CHAPTER SIXTEEN

I was lying on the straw mattress, covered by a single blanket. I was aware of being cold but I didn't really feel it. I was feeling distinctly numb and vague.

Karen was sitting on the chair beside the bed, with her feet on the top of the table. She was watching me from behind her plastic mask—the mask that looked like a transparent extra skin.

"Hi," I said, weakly.

"Welcome back," she replied. Her voice was heavy with irony. I presumed that she was annoyed with me for some reason.

"What happened?" I asked.

"What do you think happened? They pretended to be the Spanish Inquisition. You told them everything they wanted to know. You didn't hold back a thing. Which is more than can be said for your dealings with us."

"Oh," I said. "What did I tell them that I hadn't mentioned to you?"

"Something about the mutation rate of the parasite giving it the evolutionary capacity to cope with anything we can make to attack it. Or, to put it another way, even with all the resources of the lab we can't fight this thing effectively. Now if you'd told Nathan that...."

"I don't know for certain that it's true," I said, defensively. "It's just a conjecture. The only way to be sure...."

"...would be to try. But doesn't it occur to you that if you'd spilled this previously Nathan wouldn't have been so ready to believe in Sorokin's story about immunity? And doesn't it occur to you that you might have shown a much healthier dose of skepticism? If you'd been as open and honest with us as you were with them, we might not be in this mess?"

I groaned a little, more for effect than because I felt the need. "The mutation factor is a long-term thing," I told her. "Immunity would take time to break down. And there's no reason why the evolutionary potential of the parasite should make the Ego and his friends blasé about the capabilities of our lab. If we did manage to find something to attack the parasite we could do it very effectively, in the short term. In a couple of hundred years the parasite might win back its infective potential.... But that'd be far too late for the Self and the Nation. The whole thing would have to start all over from scratch, with a new generation."

"Well," she said, "they didn't look scared to me."

I tried to sit up, but it was too uncomfortable. "It all depends on how much conscious and direct control they have over the versatility of the parasite cells," I said. "I don't know... and maybe they don't until they're pushed. It's possible they can react directly against any attack we might make, without waiting for the laborious routine of mutation and natural selection. If they can...well, all bets are off anyhow. There's nothing we can do. It's bombs or nothing. Personally, I'd favor nothing, but I harbor dire suspicions about my fellow men. Especially the political species."

"You don't have to go through the routine," she said. "I know all about your prejudices.

"I never believed in truth serum," I told her, changing the subject. "I thought it was one of those attractive myths, like the philosopher's stone and the elixir of life. I thought lying was built into the way the mind works."

"Well, you were wrong. I doubt if any human being in the entire history of the race has ever been so utterly frank for such a long period of time as you were over the last couple of hours."

"They know all about Nathan's thinking on the subject?"

"They do," she confirmed. "And they got a blow-by-blow account of our rather bitter conversation of the other night, with all lurid quotes intact. You come up smelling of roses, of course. I shouldn't be surprised if they make you an honorary member. But they now have a very jaundiced view of Nathan and the UN, thanks to your big mouth."

"Ah well," I muttered. "Maybe the serum just preys on one's inner need to confess. Good for the soul, they say. Doesn't do a lot for the body, mind. And I had one hell of a nightmare."

"Tough," she said, unsympathetically.

"What are they going to do about it, now that they know?" I asked.

"Guess Who is deciding," she replied. It was the obvious answer. One big orgy of holding hands and swapping circles... thoughts going back and forth through the great network. What kind of decision might the average supermind make, given all the data I could make available to it?

Who could know?

"It doesn't make sense," I said, ruminatively. I tried to sit up again, but couldn't. I decided that the failure was an annoyance, and gathered both my wits and my strength for one big surge. Using the back of the chair for leverage I managed to pull myself up. Karen nearly fell over backwards, but managed to save herself by grabbing the table firmly.

"What doesn't?" she asked.

"Truth serum. It makes no sense at all. What do they need a truth serum for? They haven't got any secrets.... They all have access to one another's minds. In fact, they all have the same mind, to some degree. Unless there's a much greater reservoir of individuality than I'd assumed."

"You don't have places like this where there's perfect harmony," observed Karen.

That was true enough. The existence of cells suggests that occasionally people get put in them. And the Servant, when he'd told me he was letting me go, had commented that if it were a wrong decision he'd be punished for it. The way the Ego spoke made it obvious that some degree of individual initiative remained...and where there's initiative there's waywardness. It seemed that the people of the city were slightly more than just units of a super-organism. More like units of a super-community, where individual cells still retained viability and a degree of independence, potential if not actual. Which made sense.

"But why the truth serum?" I asked, again. "Mind-to-mind links cut out a lot of the potential for deception. We know that because we have Mariel. She can read discrepancies between words and thoughts. The link-up between brains must allow these people communication at least to her level of facility. And they have no *reason* to lie to one another, or to pry one another's secrets loose. They can't have developed the drug *as* a truth serum. Either it was an accidental discovery, or simply part of a whole series of discoveries.... Which implies that they must have done a lot of work on psychotropics in general. Which implies, in turn, that they may have a lot of other cute little biochemical tricks up their sleeve."

"So what?" said Karen. "Is there any particular point in this chase?"

"I don't know," I said. "I'm just trying to understand."

"Is it going to help us get out of this mess?"

As usual, she wanted to get to the heart of the matter instead of farting around the periphery. I couldn't blame her.

"It isn't," I agreed. "But nothing is. We are, as they say, at the mercy of the unpredictable. Back at the ship, all kinds of possibilities are still open, but for you and me...."

I didn't go on.

"I don't know why I come along with you on these jaunts," she said. "It always ends up like this."

It was an unfair comment, but I couldn't be bothered objecting.

"Look at it this way," I remarked. "At least we'll go together."

"I *am* looking at it that way," she assured me. "It's the thought that we might end up much more together than we ever dreamed of that worries me."

"The gods are always against you," I reminded her, "but sometimes.... The ancient Egyptians, you know, had a whole theory of eschatology based on procedures that a dead soul could adopt in order to answer the courts of divine judgment appropriately and get into heaven regardless of its actual record on Earth...a whole religion of lying to the gods and cheating one's way into heaven. The *Book of the Dead* consists almost entirely of good advice on how to put one over on the gods."

"Thanks," she said. "I really wanted to know that. Or does the story have a moral?"

"Not exactly," I told her. "It's a pretty immoral story."

Rumor has it that it is a terrible thing to fall into the hands of the living God. And that was where we seemed to be.

As if to emphasize the point, the bolts were drawn back and the door opened. It was, of course, the Ego.

The Self, apparently, had reached its decision. It hadn't taken very long. Karen didn't bother to get up and offer him the chair.

"It is settled," he said, his thin, reedy voice striking its usual high note. "Will you come with me, please."

I didn't like the sound of that *please*. It wasn't the way he usually talked.

"Where to?" I asked.

"The pyramid. It will be more comfortable. We may talk."

"Just talk?"

"There is no longer any need to be afraid," he said. "The Self now has a much more accurate appraisal of the situation. It has been decided that we should no longer attempt to adopt you into the Nation."

"Does that mean you're going to let us go?" asked Karen, suspiciously.

"Certainly," he said. "When we have made certain things clear to you. Our interests coincide precisely with your own. We wish to avoid disaster. No one wants war. Even Nathan Parrick would rather have peace."

"Sure," I said. "On his terms. I see your point.... You don't want to be bombed out of existence, which is what will surely happen unless you can come up with something very clever indeed. But you're left with the problem Nathan handed to me. How do you persuade him that you offer no threat, in the long term, to Earth and the other colony-worlds?"

"Come with me," he said. "I will explain to you what you must say. We must trust one another. I will show you how we might build such trust. And I will show you, too, how you can save your mission and renew Earth's interest in the star worlds."

I just gaped. For a moment or two, my only thought was: *pull the other one, it has bells on.*

But then I saw what I hadn't seen before, and realized exactly where there might be potential for saving this godawful situation. I saw, clear as day, just what we had to do to save the *status quo* and stop both sides from embarking upon a path of policy that might lead to ultimate ruin.

"Lead the way," I said. "I think this is going to be worth listening to."

CHAPTER SEVENTEEN

I dismounted, and gave the ox a cheerful pat on the back. Then I went to help Karen down. She was still in her plastic suit, but I'd seen no reason to reassume mine.

The oxen moved back to rejoin the third, on which the dark-skinned Servant still sat. He turned his mount away, and without any salute of farewell he began to make his way downhill again, the two riderless beasts following.

I dumped my pack on the ground and took out the radio.

"All right, Nathan," I said. "We're here. We'll keep a nice safe distance. There's not a bowman for miles and there are no cards up my sleeve. Come on out."

The airlock opened. Nathan and Mariel came out together. They were both suited up.

And Nathan was carrying a gun.

I hadn't told him much over the radio. I wanted the whole issue thrashed out face to face. I wanted him to be able to see me, and for Mariel to be there too, to assure him that I was me, the whole me, and nothing but me. I had assured him that everything would be all right. He didn't believe me. Yet.

"I'm sorry, Alex," said Nathan, moving the gun a little to show me what he was talking about. "We have to be sure. I don't know what kind of a risk is tolerable, but in a situation like this any risk at all is too much."

He stayed back beside the open airlock. Karen and I walked toward him. When we were twelve feet away he said: "That's enough."

Mariel came forward, alone. She came right up to me, looking hard into my eyes.

"I'm all right," I said. "Everything is okay."

She touched my cheeks lightly with a plastic-clad forefinger. I don't think it added anything to the effectiveness of what she was trying to do, but it gave her a little more confidence. It was a kind of ritual.

She turned away from me to look at Karen. Karen didn't say anything.

Mariel turned back, and nodded to Nathan. It was a nod that had a lot to say.

"Stay where you are," said Nathan. "They fooled her once before."

"But she *knows* us," objected Karen. "And she's not looking at us through a camera."

"You're still going to have to persuade me," said Nathan. "And whatever you have to say, it had better be good."

"Are you implying that you'd use that gun?" I asked, feeling quite relaxed. "Or just that you'd be prepared to abandon us?"

"I'll do whatever is necessary," said Nathan. "I'd hate doing it, but I'd do it."

"That's professionalism," I said.

"This isn't a good time for jokes," he observed.

"That's why I'm trying to be funny," I told him. "How would you be certain it's me unless I tried to be funny when it isn't the time?"

He conceded me a wry grin. "Yeah," he said, noncommittally.

"With friends like ours," muttered Karen, "nobody needs enemies."

"They don't know we're friends," I said. "We were silent for a *long* time. Then we called in and announced that Sorokin was bait in a trap we'd walked straight into, that we were in the city and had spilled *everything*, and that we were coming home because everything in the garden was rosy and everything would be just fine, happy ending guaranteed. They're as suspicious as hell...and who wouldn't be?"

"But we're going to listen," said Nathan, with a face that would have done credit to a poker player. "And we even came outside to do it. That's how badly we want to hear an answer, if you can persuade us that there's one available. But we want to keep the risk to a minimum. I'm making no promises. Unless you can tell us exactly why they let you go...why they haven't taken all the chances they've had...."

"Because they're afraid of us," I said. "Because they're just about as scared of us as we are of them. Their first thought was to lie to us, cheat us, and capture or destroy us. Just as our first thought was to lie to them, cheat them, and destroy them or render them harmless. They now see things in a more reasonable manner. It's our turn to do the same.

"I'll tell you why some of our fears are groundless, though that's a minor point because there's no way I can prove it to you. These people aren't embarked upon a historical course that will bring them a spaceship-building technology in two hundred years as a preparatory stage in the conquest of the universe. They don't want Earth, or other worlds...and they haven't planned any historical course at all. They haven't because they realized very quickly that they can't. They can't predict what they'll be doing in fifty years' time because they don't know what they'll *be* in fifty years' time. They hardly know what they'll be the day after tomorrow. They know very little about what they are now. The Self is only just beginning to discover the things it can do, the things it can hope to be. Its development as an entity is utterly unpredictable. It's like a little child first beginning to be aware of itself and the world that contains it. The only guides it has so far had have misled it, because the guides were the legacy of Earth, meant to pertain to beings of a radically different kind—to individuals, not to a collective communal entity. The Self isn't concerned with conquering the universe, Nathan—that's a human power fantasy, based on the urge for one individual to impose his will on others. The Self doesn't think like that. It isn't that kind of being.

"The Self isn't aiming for high technology and the creation of mechanical slaves to replace human ones. It isn't oriented in that direction at all. The Self's interest is almost exclusively itself...its only science is a species of socio-psychology that we simply don't have because it would be meaningless to us. The nearest we could ever come to it is in the most unrealistic of our Utopian fantasies, imagining a state of social life impossible of practical realization. That's where the Self started.... That was the only place it had to start. But the City of the Sun was only square one—a conceptual base from which to begin. The walls still stand, but imaginatively and existentially the Self is a long way from that now, and getting further away with every day that passes. It's already beyond our comprehension. If you want a judgment based on what the Ego has tried to convey to me, the people of the city have more individual responsibility than we feared, but also participate far more fully in collective experience than we believe to be compatible with the first notion.

"These people aren't really people any more, Nathan. What the Self is now is an alien being, in every sense of the word. Sure, it evolved out of humanity, but humanity has ancestors that were apes and insectivores and reptiles and. mud-skipping fish. It took us millions of years to become what we are instead of mud-skipping fish, but in mental terms I think the Self may have come just as far in a few short decades. You can't measure its kinship with our kind of humanity in years or generations—you have to measure it in terms of change.

"All that's obvious, but we never tried to take into account its implications. We were stuck with the thought that these people were intrinsically human but had somehow been de-humanized...that although they were now alien they retained inside them the essence of humanity. And because of that we saw what had happened to them as pure evil. If we hadn't kept on thinking of them as dehumanized, as perverted humanity, we'd never have let our minds fill up as they did with images of horror and nightmares about the conquest of the universe and defense by blanket nuclear bombing. Those ideas would never have entered our head if we'd only seen these aliens—this alien—for what it really is...something that is completely different.

"If we'd accepted the Self's alienness from the start—if we only *could* have accepted it, somehow—then we would have come out of the ship determined to make contact, to make peace, to establish friendly relations. We'd have been determined to understand it, as far as we could, but we would have known that we *couldn't* expect to fully understand. We'd have accepted what we couldn't know and couldn't find out as an inevitable reservoir of uncertainty. But because of the attitude we did bring out of the ship that reservoir became a festering pit of fear and horror. Everything that we couldn't find out became a source of danger, a *risk*. And because of our attitude, which conjured up these fears, we were on the edge of being ready to take a hand in the extinction of all life on this world.

"If you want to be cynical you can say that we can afford to take a benevolent attitude to aliens like the salamen. You can say that the only reason our attitude to the category 'alien' is positive and constructive is that our explorers have never yet found anything alien which poses any kind of a threat to us. You can say that this is different because it *does* seem to pose a threat and that no amount of talking will take away that threat or overcome the risk we'd be taking in not trying to destroy this thing.

"If you want to take that line, I'll say 'okay.' It *is* a risk. But it's a *necessary* risk...not just here, but everywhere and anywhen. It's a chance we have to take now, and the next time, and the time after that. How can we possibly use our ability to travel between the stars if we aren't willing to take risks? How can we do *anything* in life if we aren't prepared to take chances? Life and history are nothing but long sequences of gambles, and star travel is the biggest gamble of all. There's no point in having a committee of the UN draw up rules which the universe must conform to in order to allow us to move out into it in perfect safety. What use is it for the UN to say: 'All right, we're going out to the stars, we're going to take humanity into the universe at large, but *only* if we never meet anything that we can't understand, *only* if we never meet anything we can't handle, *only* if every strange race we find is completely harmless; we'll conquer the galaxy, but only if it's a *nice* galaxy, and only if it behaves itself and doesn't come up with anything that our labs can't analyze and destroy, and only if it obeys the law of mediocrity which says that everything which exists must be pretty much the same as here. Those aren't the terms on which we can make the star worlds ours, Nathan...and I don't even believe that they're the terms we ought to hope for.

"You're frightened by what we've found here. So am I. It's possible that this is the devil's world, utterly corrupted by something evil and inimical to mankind. It's possible that this is a world of witches, committed to the destruction of everything we hold dear. It's possible that unless we burn every last ounce of living flesh on this world that we may lose everything, and that the devil will rule all of Creation. It's possible, and there's absolutely no way I can prove to you that it's not. I'm defending the witches, and automatically become suspect myself. I speak for evil, if evil it is, and therefore must be corrupted myself. There's no evidence either way because the circumstances rule out the very possibility of there *being* evidence.

"But you can't proceed on the assumptions you want to apply. It's not a viable policy for living. There's no way you can exterminate every last vestige of *risk*. You can't operate on the principle of rather burning a thousand innocent souls than allowing one minion of the devil to escape. It's not right, and it's not practical. We have to face our fears and learn to live with them, Nathan. We have to learn to control our nightmares."

Throughout the tirade Nathan stood quite impassively. He listened to every word. It went in, and it didn't just flow out of him. But he didn't move a muscle, and I knew that the outside of him spoke for the inside as well.

"I know all that, Alex," he said, quietly. "Nothing here is new. Nothing here is even solid. It's just a piece of public relations...impassioned rhetoric. I can do it, too. I *will* do it, in almost exactly the same way, back home. I'll spin such a spell that I'll win ninety percent of any audience over to your way of thinking. But public relations is like possession, Alex...it's only nine points of the law. To be able to put over a stunt like that— for it even to be worth *trying* to put over a stunt like that—*I have to have something to sell.* I know that to you, what you've said is everything that's important. As moral philosophy it may be great stuff. But I'm talking about politics and the business of *practical* persuasion.

"Sure we should face our fears. Sure you can't go through life waving a gun at everything that alarms you. But you try telling that to a man who's scared, Alex. Try telling it to the man with the gun. He isn't going to be convinced, no matter how *right* you are. You have to give him something different. You have to hit his hard head with something just as hard. I'm scared, Alex. I'm playing the part of the man with the gun. And I'm afraid you're going to have to show me something that will penetrate a thick skull. You'll have to convince me that I can take what you give me back to Earth and into the UN committee rooms...and you have to persuade me that what you have will work *there,* where all the moral philosophy in the world wouldn't win the flicker of an eyebrow."

I knelt down, and I took something out of the pack. It was a small plastic phial—a specimen bottle that had been in a pocket of the packsack when Karen had first picked it up before we left the ship. Now it contained a viscous liquid, milky and lumpy, like runny porridge.

I held it up so that it caught the light.

"What is it?" he asked.

"Truth serum," I told him.

"So what?"

"I'm down to Earth now," I said. "I'm talking practical matters. What's the one force that's always guaranteed to overcome fear even in the most committeefied mind in the world?"

"Greed," he said.

I knew he'd get it in one.

"But there's no way to save the situation that way," he went on. "Even if we desperately needed a truth serum more than anything else in the universe, there's no way you could set up a claim for this world because of its trade potential. You know as well as I do that you just can't carry goods over interstellar distances. There's no way it can be made economically feasible. Not for a truth serum...or anything else."

"How about the elixir of life?" I asked.

"They have the elixir of life?"

"No," I said. "Not yet."

And then he got the point. He'd been a little slow. I'd been even slower...but I hadn't had the benefit of such direct prompting.

"You *can* run interstellar trade," I said, wanting to say it before he could dive in and steal all my lines. "We already do it. The *Daedalus* brings help to the colony worlds. But it's not material help. It's all in the head, with a little extra facility laid on in the form of a lab. The one thing you can exchange is *knowledge*...the most basic wealth of all. None of the other colonies have it, or can be expected to develop any worth exporting for hundreds of years. They're all living on the legacy of Earth, and they won't get into new patterns of discovery until they've used up that legacy in transforming their environment. But Arcadia is different. Arcadia is already into new discoveries...whole new *kinds* of discovery. They have opportunities we could never have, because they're not the same kind of beings we are. They won't do much in physics or raw chemistry—not for a long time and maybe not ever. But in biochemistry and in psychochemistry they have facilities for experiment we can never have. This is just a truth serum. We already have ways of getting at or near the truth...and maybe it won't be long before someone finds a way of countering this one. It's not particularly important. It's not worth much in terms of propaganda and getting into thick skulls.

"But tell the hardheaded men with guns that they'll be blowing up something that has potential enough to produce cures for every ill known to mankind—ills that even our advanced knowledge in genetic engineering hasn't beaten or even subdued. Tell them that they'll be blowing up something that might one day be able to offer us immortality...a way to make the human body keep renewing itself forever. Tell them that they'll be blowing up something that could eventually lead us to a full knowledge of the nature of death, and how to overcome it."

That gun was still pointing at my midriff.

"Does he mean it?" asked Nathan, quietly, of Mariel.

It wasn't really a necessary question.

"He means it," she replied. "And I think he's telling the truth."

CHAPTER EIGHTEEN

There are risks and risks. Some risks aren't worth taking simply because they're so consummately easy to counter. And that's why I had to put on yet another plastic suit in the decontamination lock. I was condemned to wearing it for a month. As a precaution. It was a sort of cruel joke by which Nathan paid me back for winning the day. He can't have taken that much joy in it. What's sauce for the goose *etc.* I insisted that if I was going to have to seal myself away from the world, so was he. As a precaution, of course. Karen got stuck with it as well...on the grounds that we couldn't be sure that her suit (and her being) hadn't been tampered with while we were prisoners in the city. It was all a bit of a farce.

Being in a suit is no fun. You can't eat properly, sterilized drinks usually taste foul, and there are other pleasures which become downright impossible. There was a certain amount of frustration attendant upon our precautions.

Nevertheless, I still went to Karen's cabin later that night, for a modest orgy of self-satisfaction in the absence of any other kind. It was good to be together, for the company.

"I was worried," she confessed to me. "I was really scared. I didn't really think you could persuade him that we were okay after they'd had us incommunicado for so long and after you told them about Sorokin changing back into a Servant. I have to hand it to you...you really talked a ring round Nathan."

"He'd have let us back in anyhow," I told her. "Even without the serum and the clever chat. He'd have taken the chance in the end."

"I'm not so sure. He can be tough."

"Sure," I said. "When we were all inside, and there was only a world beyond the airlock...then he could be tough. We could have flown away and left nothing behind, and stood by with clean hands while the UN debated butchery. We could have kept our consciences under control. Even me—if it had come to the crunch I would have rationalized it, excused it, told myself not to care more than I could bear. That's the way minds work. But once there were two of us outside, so that in order to take the big decision Nathan would have had to desert us.... Well, the odds were always in our favor. We're neither of us particularly lovable. I'm obsessive and you're a bit of a bitch. But in four years we've become part and parcel of the people in there. They've grown accustomed to us. They wouldn't abandon us if they could rationalize a policy that would allow them to save us. They'd take the risks...for us."

"You have far too much faith in human nature," she said.

"I don't have any at all," I assured her. "But I know what motives are made of."

"What would have happened," she asked pensively, "if it hadn't been you that went with Sorokin? Suppose it had been Nathan? Would they still have been so ready to play it straight after they'd heard *his* version of the whole truth and nothing but? And even if they still wanted to play the difficult way... would they have persuaded him?"

"I don't know," I replied. "But with me aboard the ship...you and he outside...."

"Everyone's expendable."

"To the UN. Not to me. Not even to Nathan. Nor to you, though you'd be damned before admitting it."

"Sure," she said dryly.

"I wouldn't even abandon the devil's advocate," I said, with all the generosity I could find. My soul was overflowing with generosity at that particular point in time. Other times, I might have thought differently about everything.

"Who?" she inquired.

"Whoever the UN put aboard to prepare the opposition case. Nathan pointed out to me that there had to be one, and I accept the logic. It's not him, or me, or Mariel. I don't believe it's Conrad or Pete, either. Conrad was out on the first trip and Pete doesn't take enough interest. That leaves you or Linda. Mariel knows, of course, but she won't tell."

"And you expect me to clear up the mystery for you? Suppose I said it wasn't me...how could you possibly believe me? And suppose it was me...what do you propose to do about it?"

"Nothing," I assured her. "Nothing at all. And you don't have to give me an answer."

"I don't intend to," she said. She lay herself back on the bed, staring up at the ceiling. I stretched out beside her, and we *both* stared up at the ceiling. That was as far as it went.

"It's true what they say," she said. "God does move in very mysterious ways.

"Sure," I agreed. "And we should all do our level best to imitate him."

ABOUT THE AUTHOR

Brian Stableford was born in Yorkshire in 1948. He taught at the University of Reading for several years, but is now a full-time writer. He has written many science-fiction and fantasy novels, including *The Empire of Fear*, *The Werewolves of London*, *Year Zero*, *The Curse of the Coral Bride*, *The Stones of Camelot*, and *Prelude to Eternity*. Collections of his short stories include a long series of *Tales of the Biotech Revolution*, and such idiosyncratic items as *Sheena and Other Gothic Tales* and *The Innsmouth Heritage and Other Sequels*. He has written numerous nonfiction books, including *Scientific Romance in Britain, 1890-1950*; *Glorious Perversity: The Decline and Fall of Literary Decadence*; *Science Fact and Science Fiction: An Encyclopedia*; and *The Devil's Party: A Brief History of Satanic Abuse*. He has contributed hundreds of biographical and critical articles to reference books, and has also translated numerous novels from the French language, including books by Paul Féval, Albert Robida, Maurice Renard, and J. H. Rosny the Elder.

www.ingramcontent.com/pod-product-compliance
Lightning Source LLC
Chambersburg PA
CBHW050742250626
47155CB00005B/1882